"So when were you going to tell me that you were pregnant?" Kruz demanded.

"You seem more concerned about my faults than our child. There were so many times when I wanted to tell you…. I don't want to argue with you about this, Kruz. I want to discuss what has happened while we've got the chance. For God's sake, Kruz, what's wrong with you? Anyone would think you were trying to drive me away—taking your child with me."

"You'll stay here until I tell you to go," he said, snatching hold of her arm.

"Let me go!" Romy cried furiously.

"There's nowhere for you to go. There's just thousands of miles of nothing out there."

"I'm leaving Argentina—"

"And then what?" he demanded.

"And then I make a life for me and our baby—the baby you don't care to acknowledge."

Was that a flicker of something human in his eyes? Had she got through to him at last? His grip had relaxed on her arm.

All about the author...
Susan Stephens

SUSAN STEPHENS was a professional singer before meeting her husband on the tiny Mediterranean island of Malta. In true Presents style they met on Monday, became engaged on Friday and were married three months later. Almost thirty years and three children later they are still in love. (Susan does not advise her children to return home one day with a similar story, as she may not take the news with the same fortitude as her own mother!)

Susan had written several nonfiction books when fate took a hand. At a charity costume ball there was an after-dinner auction. One of the lots, "Spend a Day with an Author," had been donated by Presents author Penny Jordan. Susan's husband bought this lot, and Penny was to become not just a great friend, but a wonderful mentor who encouraged Susan to write romance.

Susan loves her family, her pets, her friends and her writing. She enjoys entertaining, travel and going to the theatre. She reads, cooks and plays the piano to relax, and can occasionally be found throwing herself off mountains on a pair of skis or galloping through the countryside.

Visit Susan's website: www.susanstephens.net. She loves to hear from her readers all around the world!

Other titles by Susan Stephens available in ebook:

Harlequin Presents®

Susan Stephens

TAMING THE LAST ACOSTA

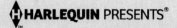

Recycling programs
for this product may
not exist in your area.

ISBN-13: 978-0-373-23896-5

TAMING THE LAST ACOSTA

Copyright © 2013 by Susan Stephens

Printed in U.S.A.

TAMING THE LAST ACOSTA

For Joanne, who holds my hand when
I'm in the dentist's chair.

CHAPTER ONE

TWO PEOPLE IN the glittering wedding marquee appeared distanced from the celebrations. One was a photojournalist, known as Romy Winner, for whom detachment was part of her job. Kruz Acosta, the brother of the groom, had no excuse. With his wild dark looks, barely mellowed by formal wedding attire, Romily—who preferred to call herself no-nonsense Romy—thought Kruz perfectly suited to the harsh, unforgiving pampas in Argentina where this wedding was taking place.

Trying to slip deeper into the shadows, she stole some more shots of him. Immune to feeling when she was working, this time she felt excitement grip her. Not just because every photo editor in the world would pay a fortune to get their hands on her shots of Kruz Acosta, the most elusive of the notorious Acosta brothers, but because Kruz stirred her in some dark, atavistic way, involving a violently raised heartbeat and a lot of ill-timed appreciation below the belt.

Perhaps it was his air of menace, or maybe it was his hard-edged warrior look, but whatever it was she was enjoying it.

All four Acosta brothers were big, powerful men, but rumours abounded where Kruz was concerned, which made him all the more intriguing. A veteran of Special Forces, educated in both Europe and America, Kruz was believed to work for two governments now, though no one really knew anything about him other than his success in business and his prowess on the polo field.

She was getting to know him through her camera lens at this wedding of Kruz's older brother, Nacho, to his beautiful blind bride, Grace. What she had learned so far was less than reassuring: Kruz missed nothing. She ducked out of sight as he scanned the sumptuously decorated wedding venue, no doubt looking for unwanted visitors like her.

It was time to forget Kruz Acosta and concentrate on work, Romy told herself sternly, even if he *was* compelling viewing to someone who made her living out of stand-out shots. It would take more than a froth of tulle and a family reunion to soften Kruz Acosta, Romy guessed, as she ran off another series of images she knew Ronald, her editor at *ROCK!*, would happily give his eye teeth for.

Just one or two more and then she'd make herself scarce…

Maybe sooner rather than later, Romy concluded

as Kruz glanced her way. This job would have been a pleasure if she'd had an official press pass, but *ROCK!* was considered a scandal sheet by many, so no one from *ROCK!* had received an invitation to the wedding. Romy was attending on secret business for the bride, on the understanding that she could use some of the shots for other purposes.

Romy's fame as a photographer had reached Grace through Holly Acosta, one of Romy's colleagues at *ROCK!* The three women had been having secret meetings over the past few months, culminating in Grace declaring that she would trust no one but Romy to make a photographic record of her wedding for her husband, Nacho, and for any children they might have. Inspired by the blind bride's courage, Romy had agreed. Grace was fast becoming a friend rather than just another client, and this was a chance in a million for Romy to see the Acostas at play—though she doubted Kruz would be as accommodating as the bride if he caught her.

So he mustn't catch her, Romy determined, shivering with awareness as she focused her lens on the one man in the marquee her camera loved above all others. He had a special sort of energy that seemed to reach her across the crowded tent, and the menace he threw out was alarming. The more shots she took of him, the more she couldn't imagine that much got in his way. It was easy to picture Kruz as a rebellious youth who had gone on to win medals for gallantry in the Special Forces. All the bespoke tailoring in the world couldn't hide the fact that Kruz Acosta was a weapon in disguise. He now ran a formidably successful security company, which placed him firmly in charge of security at this wedding.

A flush of alarm scorched her as Kruz's gaze swept over her like a searchlight and moved on. He must have seen her. The question was: would he do anything about it? She hadn't come halfway across the world in order to return home to London empty-handed.

Or to let down the bride, Romy concluded as she moved deeper into the crowd. This commission for Grace was more of a sacred charge than a job, and she had no intention of being distracted by one of the most alarming-looking men it had ever been her pleasure to photograph. Running off a blizzard of shots, she realised Kruz couldn't have stood in starker contrast to the bride. Grace's gentle beauty had never seemed more pronounced than at this moment, when she was standing beneath a flower-bedecked canopy between her husband and Kruz.

Romy drew a swift breath when the man in question stared straight at her. Lowering her camera, she glanced around, searching for a better hiding place, but shadows were in short supply in the brilliantly lit tent. One of the few things Grace could still detect after a virus had stolen her sight was light, so the dress code for the wedding was 'sparkle' and every corner of the giant marquee was floodlit by fabulous Venetian chandeliers.

Mingling with the guests, Romy kept her head down. The crowd was moving towards the receiving line, where all the Acostas were standing. There was a murmur of anticipation in the queue—and no wonder. The Acostas were an incredibly good-looking family. Nacho, the oldest brother, was clearly besotted by his beautiful new bride, while the sparks flying between Diego and his wedding planner wife Maxie could have ignited a fire. The supremely cool Ruiz Acosta clearly couldn't wait to get his firebrand wife, Romy's friend and colleague Holly, into bed, judging by the looks they were exchanging, while Lucia Acosta, the only girl in this family of four outrageously good-looking brothers, was flirting with her husband Luke Forster, the ridiculously photogenic American polo player.

Which left Kruz...

The only unmarried brother. So what? Her camera loved him, but that didn't mean *she* had to like him—though she would take full advantage of his distraction as he greeted his guests.

Those scars... That grim expression... She snapped away, knowing that everything about Kruz Acosta should put her off, but instead she was spellbound.

From a safe distance, Romy amended sensibly, as a pulse of arousal ripped through her.

And then he really did surprise her. As Kruz

turned to say something to the bride his expression softened momentarily. That was the money shot, as it was known in the trade. It was the type of unexpected photograph that Romy was so good at capturing and had built her reputation on.

She was so busy congratulating herself she almost missed Kruz swinging round to stare at her again. Now she knew how a rabbit trapped in headlights felt. When he moved she moved too. Grabbing her kitbag, she stowed the camera. Her hands were trembling as panic mounted inside her. She hurried towards the exit, knowing this was unlike her. She was a seasoned pro, not some cub reporter—a thick skin came with the job. And why such breathless excitement at the thought of being chased by him? She was hardly an innocent abroad where men were concerned.

Because Kruz was the stuff of heated erotic dreams and her body liked the idea of being chased by him. Next question.

Before she made herself scarce there were a few more shots she wanted to take for Grace. Squeezing herself into a small gap behind a pillar, she took some close-ups of flowers and trimmings—richly scented white roses and lush fat peonies in softest pink, secured with white satin ribbon and tiny silver bells. The ceiling was draped like a Bedouin tent, white and silver chiffon lavishly decorated with scented flowers, crystal beads and fiery diamanté.

Though Grace couldn't see these details the wedding planner had ensured she would enjoy a scent sensation, while Romy was equally determined to make a photographic record of the day with detailed descriptions in Braille alongside each image.

'Hello, Romy.'

She nearly jumped out of her skin, but it was only a famous celebrity touching her arm, in the hope of a photograph. Romy's editor at *ROCK!* loved those shots, so she had to make time for it. Shots like these brought in the money Romy so badly needed, though what she really longed to do was to tell the story of ordinary people in extraordinary situations through her photographs. One day she'd do that, she vowed stepping forward to take the shot, leaving herself dangerously exposed.

The queue of guests at the receiving line was thinning as people moved on to their tables for the wedding feast, and an icy warning was trickling down her spine before she even had a chance to say goodbye to the celebrity. She didn't need to check to know she was being watched. She usually managed to blend in with the crowd, with or without an official press pass, but there was nothing usual in any situation when Kruz Acosta was in town.

As soon as the celebrity moved on she found another hiding place behind some elaborate table decorations. From here she could observe Kruz to her heart's content. She settled down to enjoy the play of muscle beneath his tailored jacket and imagined him stripped to the buff.

Nice...

The only downside was Grace had mentioned that although Kruz felt at home on the pampas he was going to open an office in London—'Just around the corner from *ROCK!*,' Grace had said, as if it were a good thing.

Now she'd seen him, Romy was sure Kruz Acosta was nothing but trouble.

But attractive... He was off-the-scale *hot*.

But she wasn't here to play make-believe with one of the lead characters at this wedding. She had got what she needed and she was out of here.

Glancing over her shoulder, she noticed that Kruz was no longer in the receiving line.

So where the hell was he?

She scanned the marquee, but there was no sign of Kruz anywhere. There were quite a few exits from the tent—he could have used any one of them. She wasn't going to take any chances, and would head straight for the press coach to send off her copy. Thank goodness Holly had given her a key.

The press coach wasn't too far. She could see its twinkling lights. She quickened her step, fixing her gaze on them, feeling that same sense of being hunted—though why was she worried? She could look after herself. Growing up small and plain had ruled out girlie pursuits, so she had taken up kick-boxing instead. Anyone who thought they could take her camera was in for a big surprise.

He had recognised the girl heading towards the exit. There was no chance he would let her get away. Having signed off the press passes personally, he knew Romy Winner didn't appear on any of them.

Romy Winner was said to be ruthless in pursuit of a story, but she was no more ruthless than he was. Her work was reputed to be cutting-edge and insightful—he'd even heard it said that as a photojournalist Romy Winner had no equal—but that didn't excuse her trespass here.

She had disappointed him, Kruz reflected as he closed in on her. Renowned for lodging herself in the most ingenious of nooks, he might have expected to find Ms Winner hanging from the roof trusses, or masquerading as a waitress, rather than skulking in the shadows like some rent-a-punk oddity, with her pale face, thin body, huge kohl-ringed eyes and that coal-black, gel-spiked, red-tipped hair, for all the wedding guests to stare at and comment on.

So Romy could catch guests off-guard and snap away at her leisure?

Maybe she wasn't so dumb after all. She must have captured some great shots. He was impressed by her cunning, but far less impressed by Señorita Winner's brazen attempt to gate-crash his brother's wedding. He would make her pay. He just hadn't decided what currency he was accepting today. That would depend on his mood when he caught up with her.

Romy hurried on into the darkness. She couldn't shake the feeling she was being followed, though she doubted it was Kruz. Surely he had more important things to do?

Crunching her way along a cinder path, she reasoned that with all the Acosta siblings having been raised by Nacho, after their parents had been killed in a flood, Kruz had enjoyed no softening influence from a mother—which accounted for the air of danger surrounding him. It was no more than that. Her overworked imagination could take a rest. Pausing at a crossroads, she picked up the lights and followed them. She couldn't afford to lose her nerve now. She had to get her copy away. The money Romy earned from her photographs kept her mother well cared for in the nursing home where she had lived since Romy's father had beaten her half to death.

When Romy had first become a photojournalist it hadn't taken her long to realise that pretty pictures earned pennies, while sensational images sold almost as well as sex. Her success in the field had been forged in stone on the day she was told that her mother would need full-time care for the rest of her life. From that day on Romy had been determined that her mother would have the best of care and Romy would provide it for her.

A gust of wind sweeping down from the Andes made her shudder violently. She wondered if she had ever felt more out of place than she did now. She lived in London, amidst constant bustle and noise. Here in the shadow of a gigantic mountain range everything turned sinister at night and her chest tightened as she quickened her step. The ghostly shape of the wedding tent was far behind her now, and ahead was just a vast emptiness, dotted with faint lights from the *hacienda*. There were no landmarks on the pampas and no stars to guide her. The Acosta brothers were giants amongst men, and the land they came from was on the same impressive scale. There were no boundaries here, there was only space, and the Acostas owned most of it.

Rounding a corner, she caught sight of the press coach again and began to jog. Her breath hitched in her throat as she stopped to listen. Was that a twig snapping behind her? Her heart was hammering so violently it was hard to tell. Focusing her gaze on the press coach, with its halo of aerials and satellite dishes, she fumbled for the key, wanting to have it ready in her hand—and cried out with shock as a man's hand seized her wrist.

His other hand snatched hold of her camera. Reacting purely on instinct, she launched a stinging roundhouse kick—only to have her ankle captured in an iron grip.

'Good, but not good enough,' Kruz Acosta ground out.

Rammed up hard against the motorcoach, with Kruz's head in her face, it was hard for Romy to disagree. In the unforgiving flesh, Kruz made the evidence of her camera lens seem pallid and insubstantial. He was hard like rock, and so close she could see the flecks of gold in his fierce black eyes, as well as the cynical twist on his mouth. While their gazes were locked he brought her camera strap down, inch by taunting inch, until finally he removed it from her arm and placed it on the ground behind him.

'No,' he said softly when she glanced at it.

She still made a lunge, which he countered effortlessly. Flipping her to the ground, he stood back. Rolling away, she sprang up, assuming a defensive position with her hands clenched into angry fists, and demanded that he give it up.

Kruz Acosta merely raised a brow.

'I said—'

'I heard what you said,' he said quietly.

He was even more devastating at short range. She rubbed her arm as she stared balefully. He hadn't hurt her. He had branded her with his touch.

A shocked cry sprang from her lips when he seized hold of her again. His reach was phenomenal. His grip like steel. He made no allowance for the fact that she was half his size, so now every inch of her was rammed up tight against him, and when she fought him he just laughed, saying, 'Is that all you've got?'

She staggered as Kruz thrust her away. She felt humiliated as well as angry. Now he'd had a chance to take a better look at her he wasn't impressed. And why would he be?

'How does a member of the paparazzi get in here?'

Kruz was playing with her, she suspected. 'I'm not paparazzi. I'm on the staff at *ROCK!*'

'My apologies.' He made her a mocking bow. 'So you're a fully paid-up member of the paparazzi. With your own executive office, I presume?'

'I have a very nice office, as it happens,' she lied. He was making her feel hot and self-conscious. She was used to being in control. It was going too far to say that amongst photojournalists she was accorded a certain respect, but she certainly wasn't used to being talked down to by men.

'So as well as being an infamous photojournal-ist *and* an executive at *ROCK!* magazine,' Kruz mocked, 'I now discover that the infamous Romy Winner is an expert kick-boxer.'

Her cheeks flushed red. Not so expert, since he'd blocked her first move.

'I suppose kick-boxing is a useful skill when it

comes to gate-crashing events you haven't been invited to?' Kruz suggested.

'It's one of my interests—and just as well with men like you around—'

'Men like me?' he said, holding her angry stare. 'Perhaps you and I should get on the mat in the gym sometime.'

'Over my dead body,' she fired back.

His look suggested he expected her to blink, or flinch, or even lower her gaze in submission. She did none of those things, though she did find herself staring at his lips. Kruz had the most amazing mouth—hard, yet sensual—and she couldn't help wondering what it would feel like to be kissed by him, though she had a pretty good idea...

An idea that was ridiculous! It wouldn't happen this side of hell. Kruz was one of the beautiful people—the type she liked to look at through her lens much as a wildlife photographer might observe a tiger, without having the slightest intention of touching it. Instead of drooling over him like some lovesick teenager it was time to put him straight.

'Kick-boxing is great for fending off unwanted advances—'

'Don't flatter yourself, Romy.'

Kruz's eyes had turned cold and she shivered involuntarily. There was no chance of getting her camera back now. He was good, economical with his movements, and he was fast.

Who knew what he was like as a lover...?

Thankfully she would never find out. All that mattered now was getting her camera back.

Darting round him, she tried to snatch it—and was totally unprepared for Kruz whipping the leather jacket from her shoulders. Underneath it she was wearing a simple white vest. No bra. She hardly needed one. Her cheeks fired up when he took full inventory of her chest. She could imagine the kind of breasts Kruz liked, and perversely wished she had big bouncing breasts to thrust in his face—if only to make a better job of showing her contempt than her embarrassingly desperate nipples were doing right now, poking through her flimsy top to signal their sheer, agonising frustration.

'Still want to take me on?' he drawled provocatively.

'I'm sure I could make some sort of dent in your ego,' she countered, crossing her arms over her chest. She circled round him. 'All I want is my property back.' She glanced at the camera, lying just a tantalising distance away.

'So what's on this camera that you're so keen for me not to see?' He picked it up. 'You can collect it in the morning, when I've had a chance to evaluate your photographs.'

'It's my work, and *I* need to edit it—'

'Your unauthorised work,' he corrected her.

There was no point trying to reason with this man. Action was the only option.

One moment she was diving for the camera, and the next Kruz had tumbled her to the ground.

'Now, what shall I do with you?' he murmured, his warm, minty breath brushing her face.

With Kruz pinning her to the ground, one powerful thigh planted either side of her body, her options were limited—until he yanked her onto a soft bed of grass at the side of the cinder path. Then they became boundless. The grass felt like damp ribbons beneath her skin, and she could smell the rising sap where she had crushed it. Overlaying that was the heat of a powerful, highly sexed, highly aroused man.

She should try to escape. She should put up some sort of token struggle, at least. She should remember her martial arts training and search for a weakness in Kruz to exploit.

She did none of those things. And as for that potential weakness—as it turned out it was one they shared.

As she reached up to push him away Kruz swooped down. Ravishing her mouth was a purposeful exercise, and one at which he excelled. For a moment she was too stunned to do anything, and then the sensation of being possessed, entered, controlled and plundered, even if it was only her mouth, by a man with whom she had been having fantasy sex for quite a few hours, sent her wild with excitement. She even groaned a complaint when he pulled away, and was relieved to find it was only to remove his jacket.

For such a big man Kruz went about his business with purpose and speed. His natural athleticism, she supposed, feeling her body heat, pulse and melt at the thought of being thoroughly pleasured by him. Growing up with a pillow over her head to shut out the violence at home had left her a stranger to romance and tenderness. Given a choice, she preferred to observe life through her camera lens, but when an opportunity for pleasure presented itself she seized it, enjoyed it, and moved on. She wasn't about to turn down *this* opportunity.

Pleasure with no curb or reason? Pleasure without thought of consequence?

Correct, she informed her inner critic firmly. Even the leisurely way Kruz was folding his jacket and putting it aside was like foreplay. He was so sexy. His powerful body was sexy—his hands were sexy—the wide spread of his shoulders was sexy—his shadowy face was sexy.

Kruz's confidence in her unquestioning acceptance of everything that was about to happen was so damn sexy she could lose control right now.

A life spent living vicariously through a camera lens was ultimately unsatisfactory, while this unexpected encounter was proving to be anything but. A rush of lust and longing gripped her as he held her stare. The look they exchanged spoke about need and fulfilment. It was explicit and potent. She broke the moment of stillness. Ripping off his shirt, she sent buttons flying everywhere. Yanking the fabric from the waistband of his pants, she tossed it away, exclaiming with happy shock as bespoke tailoring yielded to hard, tanned flesh. This was everything she had ever dreamed of and more. Liberally embellished with tattoos and scars, Kruz's torso was outstanding. She could hardly breathe for excitement when he found the button on her jeans and quickly dealt with it. He quickly got them down. In comparison, her own fingers felt fat and useless as she struggled with the buckle on his belt.

'Let me help you.'

Kruz held her gaze with a mocking look as he made this suggestion. It was all the aphrodisiac she needed. She cried out with excitement when his thumbs slipped beneath the elastic on her flimsy briefs to ease them down her hips. His big hands blazed a trail of fire everywhere they touched. She couldn't bear the wait when he paused to protect them both, but it was a badly needed wake-up call. The fact that this man had thought of it before she had went some way to reminding her how far she'd travelled from the safe shores she called home.

Her body overruled the last-minute qualms. Her body was one hundred per cent in favour of what was coming. Even her tiny breasts felt swollen and heavy, while her nipples were cheekily pert and obscenely hard, and the carnal pulse throbbing insistently between her legs demanded satisfaction.

Kruz had awakened such an appetite inside her she wouldn't be human if she didn't want to discover what sex could be like with someone who really knew what he was doing. She was about to find out. When Kruz stretched his length against her she could feel his huge erection, heavy and hard against her leg. And that look in his eyes—that slumberous, confident look. It told her exactly what he intended to do with her and just how much she was going to enjoy it. And, in case she was in any doubt, he now spelled out his intentions in a few succinct words.

She gasped with excitement. With hardly any experience of dating, and even less of foreplay, she was happy to hear that nothing was about to change.

CHAPTER TWO

SHE EXCLAIMED WITH shock when Kruz eased inside her. She was ready. That wasn't the problem. Kruz was the problem. He was huge.

Built to scale.

She should have known.

Her breath came in short, shocked whimpers, pain and pleasure combined. It was a relief when he took his time and didn't rush her. She began to relax.

This was good... Yes, better than good...

Releasing the shaking breath from her lungs, she silently thanked him for giving her the chance to explore such incredible sensation at her leisure. Leisure? The brief plateau lasted no more than a few seconds, then she was clambering all over him as a force swept them into a world where moving deeper, harder, rougher, fast and furious, was more than an imperative: it was essential to life.

'You okay?' Kruz asked, coming down briefly to register concern as she screamed wildly and let go.

It seemed for ever before she could answer him,

and then she wasn't sure she said anything that made sense.

'A little better, at least?' he suggested with amusement when she quietened.

'Not that much better,' she argued, blatantly asking for more.

Taking his weight on his arms, Kruz stared down at her.

It didn't get much better than this, Romy registered groggily, lost in pleasure the instant he began to move. She loved his hard, confident mouth. She loved the feeling of being full and ready to be sated. She even loved her grassy bed, complete with night sounds: cicadas chirruping and an owl somewhere in the distance hooting softly. Kruz's clean, musky scent was in her nostrils, and when she turned her head, groaning in extremes of pleasure, her bed of grass added a piquant tang to an already intoxicating mix. She was floating on sensation, hardly daring to move in case she fell too soon. She didn't want it to end, but Kruz was too experienced and made it really hard to hold on. Moving persuasively from side to side, he pushed her little by little, closer to the edge.

'Good?' he said, staring down, mocking her with his confident smile.

'Very good,' she managed on a shaking breath.

And then he did something that lifted her onto an even higher plane of sensation. Slowly withdrawing, he left her trembling and uncertain, before slowly thrusting into her again. Whatever she had imagined before was eclipsed by this intensity of feeling. It was like the first time all over again, except now she was so much more receptive and aroused. She couldn't hold back, and shrieked as she fell, shouting his name as powerful spasms gripped her.

When she finally relaxed what she realised was her pincer grip on Kruz's arms, she realised she had probably bruised him. He was holding her just as firmly, but with more care. She loved his firm grip on her buttocks, his slightly callused hands rough on her soft skin.

'I can't,' she protested as he began to move again. 'I truly can't.'

'There's no such word as *can't*,' he whispered.

Incredibly, he was right. It didn't seem possible that she had anything left, but when Kruz stared deep into her eyes it was as if he was instructing her that she must give herself up to sensation. There was no reason to disobey and she tumbled promptly, laughing and crying with surprise as she fell again.

It turned out to be just the start of her lessons in advanced lovemaking. Pressing her knees back, Kruz stared down. Now she discovered that she loved to watch him watching her. Lifting herself up, she folded her arms behind her head so she had a better view. Nothing existed outside this extreme pleasure. Kruz had placed himself at her disposal,

and to reward him she pressed her legs as wide as
they would go. He demanded all her concentration
as he worked steadily and effectively on the task
in hand.

'You really should try holding on once in a while,'
he said, smiling against her mouth.

'Why?' she whispered back.

'Try it and you'll find out,' he said.

'Will you teach me?' Her heart drummed at the
thought.

'Perhaps,' Kruz murmured.

He wasn't joking, Romy discovered as Kruz led
her through a lengthy session of tease and withdraw
until her body was screaming for release.

'Greedy girl,' he murmured with approval. 'Again?'
he suggested, when finally he allowed her to let go.

Bracing her hands against his chest, she smiled
into his eyes. For a hectic hook-up this was turning into a lengthy encounter, and she hadn't got a
single complaint. Kruz was addictive. The pleasure
he conjured was amazing. But—

'What?' he said as she turned her head away from
him.

'Nothing.' She dismissed the niggle hiding deep
in her subconscious.

'You think too much,' he said.

'Agreed,' she replied, dragging in a fast breath as
he began to move again.

Kruz didn't need to ask if she wanted more; the

answer was obvious to both of them. Gripping his iron buttocks, she urged him on as he set up a drugging beat. Tightening her legs around his waist, she moved with him—harder—faster—giving as good as she got, and through it all Kruz maintained eye contact, which was probably the biggest turn-on of all, because he could see where she was so quickly going. Holding her firmly in place, he kept her in position beneath him, and when the storm rose he judged each thrust to perfection. Pushing her knees apart, he made sure they both had an excellent view, and now even he was unable to hold on, and roared with pleasure as he gave in to violent release.

She went with him, falling gratefully into a vortex of sensation from which there was no escape. It was only when she came to that she realised fantasy had in no way prepared her for reality—her fantasies were wholly selfish, and Kruz had woken something inside her that made her care for him just a little bit. It was a shame he didn't feel the same. Now he was sated she sensed a core of ice growing around him. It frightened her, because she was feeling emotional for the first time with a man. And now he was pulling back—emotionally, physically.

No wonder that niggle of unease had gripped her, Romy reflected. She was playing well out of her league. As if to prove this, Kruz was already on his feet, pulling on his clothes. He buckled his belt as if it were just another day at the office. She might have laughed under other circumstances when he was forced to tug the edges of his shirt together where she had ripped the buttons off. He did no more than hide the evidence of her desperation beneath his tie. How could he be so chillingly unfazed by all this? Her unease grew at the thought that what had just happened between them had made a dangerously strong impression on her, while it appeared to have washed over Kruz.

And why not? What happened was freely given and freely taken by both of you.

'Are you okay?' he said, glancing down when she remained immobile.

'Of course I am,' she said in a casual tone. Inwardly she was screaming. Was she really so stupid she had imagined she would come out of something like this unscathed?

Even inward reasoning didn't help—she was still waiting for him to say something encouraging. How pathetic was that? She had never felt like this before, and had no way of dealing with the feelings, so, gathering up her clothes, she lost herself in mundane matters—shaking the grass off her jacket, pulling on her jeans, sorting her hair out, then smoothing her hands over her face, hoping that by the time she removed them she would appear cool and detached.

Wrong. She felt as if she'd come out the wrong end of a spin dry.

Her thoughts turned at last to her camera. It was

still lying on the bank, temptingly close. She had learned her lesson where lunging for it was concerned, but felt confident that Kruz would give it to her now. It was the least he could do.

Fortunately Kruz appeared to be oblivious both to her and to her camera. He was on the phone, telling his security operatives that he was patrolling the grounds.

She eased her neck, as if that would ease the other aches, most of which had taken up residence in her heart.

Hadn't she learned anything from the past? Had Kruz made her forget her father's rages and her mother's dependency on a violent man?

Kruz hadn't been in any way violent towards her—but he was strong, commanding, and detached from emotion. All the things she had learned to avoid.

She was safe in that, unlike her mother, she had learned to avoid the pitfalls of attachment by switching off her emotions. In that she wasn't so dissimilar from Kruz. This was just a brief interlude of fun for both of them and now it was over. Neither of them was capable of love.

Love?

He swung round as she made a wry sound. Love was a long road to nowhere, with a punch in the teeth at the end. So, yes, if she was in any doubt at all about the protocol between two strangers who'd just had sex on a grassy bank, she'd go with cool and detached every time.

'Right,' he said, ending the call, 'I need to get back.'

'Of course,' she said off-handedly. 'But I'd like my camera first.'

He frowned, as if they were two strangers at odds with each other. 'You've had your fun and now you're on your way,' he said.

She'd asked for that, Romy concluded. 'Well, I'm not going anywhere without it,' she said stubbornly. It was true. The camera was more than a tool of her trade, it was a fifth limb. It was an extension of her body, of her mind. It was the only way she knew how to make the money she needed to support herself and her mother.

'I've told you already. You'll get it back when I've checked it,' he said coldly, hoisting the camera over his shoulder.

'You're my censor now?' she said, chasing after him. 'I don't think so.'

The look Kruz gave her made her stomach clench with alarm.

'You can sleep in the bunkhouse,' he said, 'along with the rest of the press crew. Pick up your camera in the morning from my staff.'

She blinked. He'd said it as if they hadn't touched each other, pleasured each other.

They'd had sex and that was all.

Except for the slap in the face she got from realising that he saw it as no reason to give up her camera. 'By morning it will be too late—I need it now.'

'For what?' he said.

'I have to edit the photographs and then catch the news desk.' It was a lie of desperation, but she would do anything to recover her camera. 'There is another reason,' she added, waiting for a thunderclap to strike her down. This idea had only just occurred to her. 'I need to work on the shots I'm donating to your charity.'

As if he'd guessed, Kruz's eyes narrowed. 'The Acosta charity?'

'Yes.' She had a lot of shots in the can, Romy reasoned, quickly running through them in her mind. She had more than enough to pay for her mother's care and to keep herself off the breadline. She had taken a lot of shots specifically for Grace's album, and he couldn't have those, but there were more—plenty more.

Had she bought herself a reprieve? Romy wondered as she stared at Kruz. 'I've identified a good opportunity for the charity,' she said, as the germ of an idea sprouted wings.

'Tell me,' Kruz said impatiently.

'My editor at *ROCK!* is thinking about making a feature on the Acostas and your charity.' Or at least she would make sure he was thinking about it by the time she got back. 'Think of how that would raise the charity's profile,' she said, dangling a carrot she hoped no Acosta in his right mind could refuse.

'So why didn't Grace or Holly tell me about this?' Kruz probed, staring at her keenly. 'If either of them had mentioned it I would have made sure you were issued with an official pass.'

'I *am* here on a mission for Grace,' Romy admitted, 'which is how I got in. Grace asked me not to say anything, and I haven't. It's crucial that Nacho doesn't learn about Grace's special surprise. I hope you'll respect that.' Kruz remained silent as she went on. 'I'm sure Grace and Holly were just too wrapped up in the wedding to remember to tell you,' she said, not wanting to get either of her friends into trouble.

Kruz paused. And now she could only wait.

'I suppose Grace could confirm this if I asked her?'

'If you feel like interrogating a bride on her wedding day, I'm sure she would.'

One ebony brow lifted. Whether Kruz believed her or not, for the moment she had him firmly in check.

'The solution to this,' he remarked, 'is that *I* take a look at the shots and *I* decide.'

As he strode away she ran after him. Dodging in front of him, she forced him to stop.

He studied Romy's elfin features with a practised eye. He interpreted the nervous hand running distractedly through her disordered hair. The camera meant everything to her, and if there was one thing that could really throw Ms Winner he had it swinging from his shoulder now. She was terrified he was going to disappear with her camera. She worked with it every day. It was her family, her income stream, her life. He almost felt sorry for her, and then stamped the feeling out. What was Romy Winner to *him?*

Actually, she was a lot more than he wanted her to be. She had got to him in a way he hadn't quite fathomed yet. 'Is there some reason why I shouldn't see these shots?' he asked, teasing her by lifting the camera to Romy's eye level.

'None whatsoever,' she said firmly, but her face softened in response to his mocking expression and she almost smiled.

Testing Romy was fun, he discovered, and fun and he were strangers. With such a jaundiced palette as his, any novelty was a prize. But he wouldn't taunt her any longer. He wasn't a bully, and wouldn't intentionally try to increase that look of concern in her eyes. 'Shall we?' he invited, glancing at the press coach.

She eyed him suspiciously, perhaps wondering if she was being set up. She knew there was nothing she could do about it, if that were the case. She strode ahead of him, head down, mouth set in a stubborn line, no doubt planning her next move. And then she really did throw him.

'So, what have you got to hide?' she asked him, swinging round at the door

'Me?' he demanded.

Tilting her head to one side, she studied his face. 'People with something to hide are generally wary of me and my camera, so I wondered what *you* had to hide…'

'You think that's why I confiscated it?'

'Maybe,' she said, not flinching from his stare.

That direct look of hers asked a lot of questions about a man who could have such prolonged and spectacular sex with a woman he didn't know. It was a look that suggested Romy was asking herself the same question.

'Are you worried that I might have taken some compromising pictures of you?' she said. There was a tug of humour at one corner of her mouth.

'Worried?' He shook his head. But the truth was he had never been so reckless with a woman. He sure as hell wouldn't be so reckless again.

'Kruz?' she prompted.

His name sounded soft on her lips. That had to be a first. He smiled. 'What?'

'Just checking you know I'm still here.'

He gave her a wry look and felt a surge of heat when she tossed one back. He wasn't an animal. He was still capable of feeling. His brother Nacho had made him believe that when Kruz had been discharged from the army hospital. It was Nacho who had persuaded him to channel his particular talents into a security company, saying Kruz must need and feel and care before he could really start living again. Nacho was right. The more he looked at Romy, the more human he felt.

Did Kruz *have* to stare at her lips like that? Here she was, trying to forget her body was still thrilling from his touch, and he wasn't making it easy. She was a professional woman, trying to persuade herself she would soon get over tonight—yet all he had to do was look at her for her to long for him to take hold of her and draw her into an embrace that was neither sexual nor mocking. She had never wanted to share and trust and rest awhile quite so badly.

And she wasn't about to fall into that trap now.

'Shall we take a look?'

She looked at Kruz and frowned.

'The pictures?' he prompted, and she realised that he had not only removed the key to the press coach from her hand, but had opened the door and was holding it for her.

That yearning feeling inside…?

It wasn't helpful. Women who felt the urge to nurture men would end up like her mother: battered, withdrawn, and helpless in a nursing home.

She led the way into the coach. Her manner was cold. They were both cold, and that suited her fine.

Romy's mood now was a slap in the face to him after what they'd experienced together, but he had to concede she was only as detached as he was. He was just surprised, he supposed, that those much vaunted attributes of tenderness and sensitivity, which women were supposed to possess in abundance, appeared to have bypassed her completely. He should be pleased about that, but he wasn't. He was offended. Romy was the first woman who hadn't clung to him possessively after sex. And bizarrely, for the first time in his life, some primitive part of him had wanted her to.

'Are you coming in?' she said, when he stood at the entrance at the top of the steps.

His senses surged as he brushed past her. However unlikely it seemed to him, this whip-thin fighting girl stirred him like no other. He wanted more. So did she, judging by than quick intake of breath. He could feel her sexual hunger in the energy firing between them. But Romy wanted more that he could give her. He wanted more of Romy, but all he wanted was sex.

CHAPTER THREE

SHE MADE HER way down the aisle towards the area at the rear of the coach set aside for desks and equipment. Her small, slender shape, dressed all in black, quickly became part of the shadows.

'I know there's a light switch in here somewhere,' she said.

Her voice was a little shaky now the door was closed, and the tension rocketed between them. He could feel her anticipation as she waited for his next move. He could taste it in the air. He could detect her arousal. He was a hunter through and through.

'Here,' he said, pressing a switch that illuminated the coach and set some unseen power source humming.

'Thank you,' she said, with her back to him as she sat down at a desk.

'You'll need this,' he said, handing over the camera.

She thanked him and hugged it to her as if it contained gold bars rather than her shots.

He had more time than he needed while she logged on. He used it to reflect on what had happened over the past hour or so. Ejecting Romy from the wedding feast should have been straightforward. She should have been on her way to Buenos Aires by now, then back to London. Instead his head was still full of her, and his body still wanted her. He could still hear her moaning and writhing beneath him and feel her beneath his hands. He could still taste her on his mouth, and he could remember the smell of her soap-fresh skin. He smiled in the shadows, remembering her attacking him, that tiny frame surprisingly strong, yet so undeniably feminine. Why did Romy Winner hide herself away behind the lens of a camera?

A blaze of colour hit the screen as she began to work. What he saw answered his question. Romy Winner was quite simply a genius with a camera. Images assailed his senses. The scenery was incredible, the wildlife exotic. Her pictures of the Criolla ponies were extraordinary. She had captured some amusing shots of the wedding guests, but nothing cruel, though she *had* caught out some of the most pompous in less than flattering moments. She'd taken a lot of pictures of the staff too, and it was those shots that really told a story. Perhaps because more expression could be shown on faces that hadn't been stitched into place, he reflected dryly as Romy continued to sort and select her images.

She'd made him smile. Another first, he mused as she turned to him.

'Well?' she said. 'Do you like what you see?'

'I like them,' he confirmed. 'Show me what else you've got.'

'There's about a thousand more.'

'I'm in no hurry.' For maybe the first time in his life.

'Why don't you pull up a chair?' she suggested. 'Just let me know if there any images you don't feel are suitable for the charity.'

'So I'm your editor now?' he remarked, with some amusement after her earlier comment about censorship.

'No,' she said mildly. 'You're a client I want to please.'

He inclined his head in acknowledgement of this. He could think of a million ways she could please him. When she turned back to her work he thought the nape of her neck extremely vulnerable and appealing, just for starters. He considered dropping a kiss on the peachy flesh, and then decided no. Once he'd tasted her…

'What do you think of these?' she said, distracting him.

'Grace is very beautiful,' he said as he stared at Romy's shots of the bride. He could see that his new sister-in-law was exquisite, like some beautifully fashioned piece of china. But did Grace move him?

Did she make his blood race? He admired Grace as he might admire some priceless *objet d'art*, but it was Romy who heated his blood.

'She is beautiful, isn't she?' Romy agreed, with a warmth in her voice he had never noticed before. She certainly didn't use that voice when she spoke to him.

And why should he care?

Because for the first time in his life he found himself missing the attentions of a woman, and perhaps because he was still stung, after Romy's enthusiastic response to their lovemaking, that she wasn't telling him how she thrilled and throbbed, and all the other things his partners were usually at such pains to tell him. Had Romy Winner simply feasted on him and moved on? If she had, it would be the first time any woman had turned the tables on him.

'This is the sort of shot my editor loves,' she said as she brought a picture of him up on the screen.

'Why is that?'

'Because you're so elusive,' she explained. 'You're hardly ever photographed. I'll make a lot from this,' she added with a pleased note in her voice.

Was he nothing but a commodity?

'Though what I'd *like* to do,' she explained, 'is give it to the charity. So, much as I'd like to make some money out of you, you can have this one *gratis.*'

As she turned to him he felt like laughing. She

was so honest, he felt…uncomfortable. 'Thank you,' he said with a guarded expression. 'If you've just taken a couple of shots of me you can keep the rest. '

'What makes you think I'd want to take more than one?'

Youch.

What, indeed? He shrugged and even managed to smile at that.

Romy Winner intrigued him. He had grown up with women telling him he was the best and that they couldn't get enough of him. He'd grown up fighting for approval as the youngest of four highly skilled, highly intelligent brothers. When he couldn't beat Nacho as a youth he had turned to darker pursuits—in which, naturally, he had excelled—until Nacho had finally knocked some sense into him. Then Harvard had beckoned, encouraging him to stretch what Nacho referred to as the most important muscle in his body: the brain. After college he had found the ideal outlet for his energy and tirelessly competitive nature in the army.

'There,' Romy said, jolting him back from these musings. 'You're finished.'

'I wouldn't be too sure of that,' he said, leaning in close to study her edited version. He noticed again how lithe and strong she was, and how easy it would be to pull her into his arms.

'I have a deadline,' she said, getting back to work.

'Go right ahead.' He settled back to watch her.

The huge press coach was closing in on her, and all the tiny hairs on the back of her neck were standing erect at the thought of Kruz just a short distance away. She could hear him breathing. She could smell his warm, sexy scent. Some very interesting clenching of her interior muscles suggested she was going to have to concentrate really hard if she was going to get any work done.

'Could you pass me that kitbag?' she said, without risking turning round. She needed a new memory card and didn't want to brush past him.

Her breath hitched as their fingers touched and that touch wiped all sensible thought from her head. All she could think about now was what they had done and what they could do again.

Work!

She pulled herself back to attention with difficulty, but even as she worked she dreamed, while her body throbbed and yearned, setting up a nagging ache that distracted her.

'Shall I put this other memory card in the pocket for you?' Kruz suggested.

She realised then that she had clenched her hand over it. 'Yes—thank you.'

His fingers were firm as they brushed hers again, and that set up more distracting twinges and delicious little aftershocks. Would she ever be able to live normally again?

Not if she kept remembering what Kruz had done—and so expertly.

Her mind was in turmoil. Every nerve-ending in her body felt as if it had been jangled. And all he'd done was brush her hand!

Somehow she got through to the end of the editing process and was ready to show him what she'd got. She ran through the images, giving a commentary like one stranger informing another about this work, and even while Kruz seemed genuinely interested and even impressed she felt his aloofness. Perhaps he thought she was a heartless bitch after enjoying him so fully and so vigorously. Perhaps he thought she took *what* she wanted *when* she wanted. Perhaps he was right. Perhaps they deserved each other.

So why this yearning ache inside her?

Because she wanted things she couldn't have, Romy reasoned, bringing up a group photograph of the Acostas on the screen. They were such a tight-knit family...

'Are you sure you want to give me all these shots?'

'Concerned, Kruz?' she said, staring at him wryly. 'Don't worry about me. I've kept more than enough shots back.'

'I'd better see the ones you're giving me again.'

'Okay. No problem.' She ran through them again, just for the dangerous pleasure of having Kruz lean in close. She had never felt like this before—so aware, alert and aroused. It was like being hunted by the hunter she would most like to be caught by.

'These are excellent,' Kruz commented. 'I'm sure Grace can only be thrilled when she hears the reaction of people to these photographs.'

'Thank you. I hope so,' she said, concentrating on the screen. Grace's wedding was the first romantic project she had worked on. Romy was better known as a scandal queen. And that was one of the more polite epithets she'd heard tossed her way.

'This one I can't take,' Kruz insisted when she flashed up another image on the screen. 'You have to make *some* money,' he reminded her.

Was this a test? Was he paying her off? Or was that her insecurity speaking? He might just be making a kindly gesture, and she maybe should let him.

She shook her head. 'I can't sell this one,' she said quietly. 'I want you to have it.'

The picture in question showed Kruz sharing a smile with his sister, Lucia. It was a rare and special moment between siblings, and it belonged to them alone—not the general public. It was a moment in time that told a story about Nacho's success at bringing up his brothers and sister while he was still very young. They would see that when they studied it, just as she had. She wouldn't dream of selling something like that.

'Frame it and you'll always have a reminder of what a wonderful family you have.'

Why was she doing this for him? Kruz wondered suspiciously. He eased his shoulders restlessly, realising that Romy had stirred feelings in him he hadn't experienced since his parents were alive. He stared at her, trying to work out why. She was fierce and passionate one moment, aloof and withdrawn the next. He might even call her cold. He couldn't pretend he understood her, but he'd like to—and that was definitely a first.

'Thank you,' he said, accepting the gift. 'I appreciate it.'

'I'll make a copy for Lucia as well,' she offered, getting back to work.

'I know my sister will appreciate that.' After Lucia had picked herself off the floor because he'd given her a gift outside of her birthday or Christmas.

The tension between them had subsided with this return to business. He was Romy's client and she was his photographer—an excellent photographer. Her photographs revealed so much about other people, while the woman behind the lens guarded her inner self like a sphinx.

DAMN. She was going to cry if she didn't stop looking at images of Grace and Nacho. So that was what love looked like…

'Shall we move on?' she said briskly, because Kruz seemed in no hurry to bring the viewing session to an end. She was deeply affected by some of the shots she had captured of the bridal couple, and that wasn't helpful right now. Since she was a child she had felt the need to protect her inner self. Drawing a big, thick safety curtain around herself rather than staring at an impossible dream on the screen would be her action of choice right now.

'That was a heavy sigh,' Kruz commented.

She shrugged, neither wanting nor able to confide in him. 'I just need to do a little more work,' she said. 'That's if you'll let me stay to do it?' she added, turning to face him, knowing it could only be a matter of minutes before they went their separate ways.

This was the moment she had been dreading and yet she needed him to go, Romy realised. Staring at those photographs of Grace and Nacho had only underlined the fact that her own life was going nowhere.

'Here,' she said, handing over the memory stick. 'These are for you and for the charity. You *will* keep that special shot?' she said, her chest tightening at the thought that Kruz might think nothing of it.

'So I can stare at myself?' he suggested, slanting her a half-smile.

'So you can look at your family,' she corrected him, 'and feel their love.'

Did he *have* to stare at her so intently? She wished he wouldn't. It made her uncomfortable. She didn't know what Kruz expected from her.

'What?' she said, when he continued to stare.

'I never took you for an emotional woman,' he said.

'Because I'm not,' she countered, but her breath caught in her throat, calling her a liar. The French called this a *coup de foudre*—a thunderbolt. She had no explanation for the longing inside her except to say Kruz had turned her life inside out. It made no sense. They hardly knew each other outside of sex. They didn't know if they could trust each other, and they had no shared history. They had everything to learn about each other and no time to do so. And why would Kruz *want* to know more about her?

They could be friends, maybe...

Friends? She almost laughed out loud at this naïve suggestion from a subconscious that hadn't learned much in her twenty-four years of life. Romy Winner and Kruz Acosta? Ms Frost and Señor Ice? Taking time out to get to know each other? To *really* get to know each other? The idea was so preposterous she wasn't going to waste another second on it. She'd settle for maintaining a truce between them long enough for her to leave Argentina in one piece with her camera.

'Thanks for this,' Kruz said, angling his stubble-shaded chin as he slipped the memory stick into his pocket.

She felt lost when he turned to go—something else she would have to get used to. She had to get over him. She'd leave love at first sight to those who believed in it. As far as she was concerned love at first sight was a load of bull. Lust at first sight, maybe. Lack of self-control, certainly.

Her throat squeezed tight when he reached the door and turned to look at her.

'How are you planning to get back to England, Romy?'

'The same way I arrived, I guess,' she said wryly.

'Did you bring much luggage with you?'

'Just the essentials.' She glanced at her kitbag, where everything she'd brought to Argentina was stashed. 'Why do you ask?'

'My jet's flying to London tomorrow and there are still a few spare places, if you're stuck.'

Did he mean stuck as in unprepared? Did he think she was so irresponsible? Maybe he thought she was an opportunist who seized the moment and thought nothing more about it?

'I bought a return ticket,' she said, just short of tongue in cheek. 'But thanks for the offer.'

Kruz shrugged, but as he was about to go through the door he paused. 'You're passing up the chance to take some exclusive shots of the young royals—'

'So be it,' she said. 'I wouldn't dream of intruding on their privacy.'

'Romy Winner passing up a scoop?'

'What you're suggesting sounds more like a cheap thrill for an amateur,' she retorted, stung by his poor opinion of her. 'When celebrities or royals are out in public it's a different matter.'

Kruz made a calming motion with his hands.

'I *am* calm,' she said, raging with frustration at the thought that they had shared so much yet knew so little about each other. Kruz had tagged her with the label paparazzi the first moment he'd caught sight of her—as someone who would do anything it took to get her shots. Even have sex with Kruz Acosta, presumably, if that was what was required.

'Romy—'

'What?' she flashed defensively.

'You seem...angry?' Kruz suggested dryly.

She huffed, as if she didn't care what he thought, but even so her gaze was drawn to his mouth. 'I just wonder what type of photographer you think I am,' she said, shaking her head.

'A very good one, from what I've seen today, Señorita Winner,' Kruz said softly, completely disarming her.

'*Gracias*,' she said, firming her jaw as they stared at each other.

And now Kruz should leave. And she should stay where she was—at the back of the coach, as far away from him as possible, with a desk, a chair and most of the coach seats between them.

She waited for him to go, to close the door behind him and bring this madness to an end.

He didn't go.

Leaning over the driver's seat, Kruz hit the master switch and the lights dimmed, and then he walked down the aisle towards her.

CHAPTER FOUR

THEY COLLIDED SOMEWHERE in the middle and there was a tangle of arms and moans and tongues and heated breathing.

She kicked off her boots as Kruz slipped his fingers beneath the waistband of her jeans. The button sprang free and the zipper was down, the fabric skimming over her hips like silk, so that now she was wearing only her jacket, the white vest and her ridiculously insubstantial briefs. Kruz ripped them off. Somehow the fact that she was partly clothed made what was happening even more erotic. There was only one area that needed attention and they both knew it.

Her breathing had grown frantic, and it became even more hectic when she heard foil rip. She was working hectically on Kruz's belt and could feel his erection pressing thick and hard against her hand. She gasped with relief as she released him. She was getting better at this, she registered dazedly, though her brain was still scrambled and she was gasping for breath. Kruz, on the other hand, was breathing steadily, like a man who knew exactly where he was going and how to get there. His control turned her on. He was a rock-solid promise of release and satisfaction, delivered in the most efficient way

'Wrap your legs around me, Romy,' he commanded as he lifted her.

Kruz's movements were measured and certain, while she was a wild, feverish mess. She did as he said, and as she clung to him he whipped his hand across the desk, clearing a space for her. She groaned with anticipation as he moved between her legs. The sensation was building to an incredible pitch. She cried out encouragement as he positioned her, his rough hands firm on her buttocks just the way she liked them. Pressing her knees back, he stared into her eyes. Pleasure guaranteed, she thought, reaching up to lace her fingers through his hair, binding him to her.

This time…this one last time. And then never again.

She was so ready for him, so hungry. As Kruz sank deep, shock, pleasure, relief, eagerness, all combined to help her reach the goal. Thrusting firmly, he seemed to feel the same urgency, but then he found his control and began to tease her. Withdrawing slowly, he entered her again in the way she loved. The sensation was incredible and she couldn't hold on. She fell violently, noisily, conscious only of her own pleasure until the waves had subsided a little, when she was finally able to remember that this was for both of them. Tightening her muscles, she left Kruz in no doubt that she wasn't a silent partner but a full participant.

He smiled into her eyes and pressed her back against the desk. Wherever she took him he took her one level higher. Pinning her hands above her head, he held her hips firmly in place with his other hand as he took her hard and fast. There was no finesse and only one required outcome, and understanding the power she had over him excited her. Grabbing his arms, she rocked with him, welcoming each thrust as Kruz encouraged her in his own language. Within moments she was flying high in a galaxy composed entirely of light, with only Kruz's strong embrace to keep her safe.

It was afterwards that was awkward, Romy realised as she pulled on her jeans. When they were together they were as close as two people could be—trusting, caring, encouraging, pleasuring. But now they were apart all that evaporated, disappeared almost immediately. Kruz had already sorted out his clothes and was heading for the door. They could have been two strangers who, having fallen to earth, had landed in a place neither of them recognised.

'The seat on the jet is still available if you need it,' he said, pausing at the door.

She worked harder than ever to appear nonchalant. If she looked at Kruz, really looked at him, she would want him to stay and might even say so.

'I won't be stuck,' she said, assuming an air of confidence. 'But thanks again for the offer. And don't forget I'm only an e-mail away if you ever need any more shots from the wedding.'

'And only round the corner when I get to London,' he said opening the door.

What the hell...? She pretended not to understand. Say anything at all and her cool façade would shatter into a million pieces. When tears threatened she bit them back. She wasn't going to ask Kruz if they would meet up in London. This wasn't a date. It was a heated encounter in the press coach. And now it was nothing.

'I'll put the lights on for you,' he said, killing her yearning for one last meaningful look from Kruz.

'That would be great. Thank you.' She was proud of herself for saying this without expression. She was proud of remaining cool and detached. 'I've got quite a bit of work left to do.'

'I'll leave you to it, then,' he said. 'It's been a pleasure, Romy.'

Her head shot up. Was he mocking her?

Kruz was mocking both of them, Romy realised, seeing the tug at one corner of his mouth.

'Me too,' she called casually. After all, this was just another day in the life of a South American playboy. It didn't matter how much her heart ached because Kruz had gone, leaving her with just the flickering images of him on a computer screen for company.

Glancing back, he saw Romy through the window of the coach. She was poring over the monitor screen as if nothing had happened. She certainly wasn't watching him go. She was no clinging vine. It irked him. His male ego had taken a severe hit. He was used to women trying to pin him down, asking him when they'd meet again—if he'd call them—could they have his number? Romy didn't seem remotely bothered.

The wedding party was still in full swing as he approached the marquee. He rounded up his team, heard their reports and supervised the change-over for the next shift. All of these were measurable activities, which were a blessed relief after his encounter with the impossible-to-classify woman he'd left working in the press coach.

The woman he still wanted

Yeah, that one, he thought.

The noise coming from the marquee was boisterous, joyous, celebratory. Shadows flitted to and fro across the gently billowing tent, silhouettes jouncing crazily from side to side as the music rose and fell.

And Romy was on her own in the press coach.

So what? She was safe there. He'd get someone to check up on her later.

Stopping dead in his tracks, he swung round to look back the way he'd come. He'd send one of the men to make sure she made it to the bunkhouse safely.

Really?

Okay, so maybe he'd do that himself.

Romy shot up. Hearing a sound in the darkness, she was instantly awake. Reaching for the light on the nightstand, she switched it on. And breathed a sigh of relief.

'Sorry if I woke you,' the other girl said, stumbling over the end of the bed as she tried to kick off her shoes, unzip her dress and tumble onto the bed all at the same time. 'Jane Harlot, foreign correspondent for *Frenzy* magazine—pleased to meet you.'

'Romy Winner for *ROCK!*'

Jane stretched out a hand and missed completely. 'Brilliant—I love your pictures. Harlot's not my real name,' Jane managed, before slamming a hand over her mouth. 'Sorry—too much to drink. Never could resist a challenge, even when it comes from a group of old men who look as if they have pickled their bodies in alcohol to preserve them.'

'Here, let me help you,' Romy offered, recognising a disaster in the making. Swinging her legs over the side of the bed, she quickly unzipped her new roomie's dress. 'Did you have a good time?'

'Too good,' Jane confessed, shimmying out of

the red silk clingy number. 'Those gauchos really know how to drink. But they're chivalrous too. One of them insisted on accompanying me to the press coach and actually waited outside while I sent my copy so he could escort me back here.'

'He waited for you outside the press coach?'

'Of course outside,' Jane said, laughing. 'He was about ninety. And, anyway, it didn't take me long to send my stuff. What I write is basically a comic strip. You know the sort of thing—scandal, slebs, stinking rich people. I only got a look-in because my dad used to work with one of the reporters who got an official invitation and he brought me in as his assistant.'

Looking alarmed at this point, Jane waved a hand, keeping the other hand firmly clamped over her mouth.

Jane had landed a big scoop, and Romy was hardly in a position to criticise the other girl's methods. This wasn't a profession for shrinking violets. The Acostas had nothing to worry about, but some of their guests definitely did, she reflected, remembering those prominent personalities she had noticed attending the wedding with the wrong partner.

'Are you sure you're okay?' she asked with concern as Jane got up and staggered in the general direction of the bathroom.

'Fine…I'll sleep it off on the plane going home. The gauchos said their boss has places going spare on his private jet tomorrow, so I'll be travelling with the young royals, no less. And I'll be collected from here and taken to the airstrip in a limo. I'll be in the lap of luxury one minute and my crummy old office the next.'

'That's great—enjoy it while you can,' Romy called out, trying to convince herself that this was a good thing, that she was in fact *Saint* Romy and thoroughly thrilled for Jane, and didn't mind at all that the man she'd had sex with hadn't even bothered to see her back to the bunkhouse safely.

He stayed on post until the lights went out in the bunkhouse and he was satisfied Romy was safely tucked up in bed. Pulling away from the fencepost, it occurred to him that against the odds his caring instinct seemed to have survived. But before he could read too much into that he factored his security business into the mix. Plus he had a sister. Before Lucia had got together with Luke he had always hoped someone would keep an eye on her when he wasn't around. Why should he be any different where a girl like Romy was concerned?

London. Monday morning. The office. Grey skies. Cold. Bleak. Dark-clad people racing back and forth across the rainswept street outside her window, heads down, shoulders hunched against the bitter wind.

It might as well be raining inside, Romy thought, shivering convulsively in her tiny cupboard of an office. It was so cold.

She was cold inside and out, Romy reflected, hugging herself. She was back at work, which normally she loved, but today she couldn't settle, because all she could think about was Kruz. And what was the point in that? She should do something worthwhile to make her forget him.

Something like *this*, Romy thought some time later, poring over the finished version of Grace Acosta's wedding journal. She had added a Braille commentary beside each photograph, so that Grace could explain each picture as she shared the journal. Romy had worried about the space the Braille might take up at first but, putting herself in Grace's place, had known it was the right thing to do.

Sitting back, she smiled. She had been looking forward to this moment for so long—the moment when she could hand over the finished journal to Grace. She wasn't completely freelance yet, though this tiny office at *ROCK!* had housed many notable freelance photographers at the start of their careers and Romy dreamed of following in their footsteps. She hoped this first, really important commission for Grace would be the key to helping her on her way, and that she could make a business out of telling stories with pictures instead of pandering to the insatiable appetite for scandal. Maybe she could tell

real stories about real people with her photographs—
family celebrations, local news, romance—

Romance?

Yes. Romance, Romy thought, setting her mouth
in a stubborn line.

Excuse me for asking the obvious, but what exactly do you know about romance?

As her inner critic didn't seem to know when to
be quiet, she answered firmly: *In the absence of
romance in my own life, my mind is a blank sheet
upon which I will be able to record the happy moments in other people's lives.*

Gathering up her work, Romy headed for the editing suite run by the magazine's reining emperor
of visuals: Ronald Smith. *ROCK!* relied on photographs for impact, which made the editor one of the
most influential people in the building.

'Ronald,' Romy said, acknowledging her boss as
she walked into his hushed and perfumed sanctum.

'Well? What have you got for me, princess?' Ronald demanded, lowering his *faux*-tortoiseshell of-the-
moment spectacles down his surgically enhanced
nose.

'Some images to blow your socks off,' she said
mildly.

'Show me,' Ronald ordered.

Romy stalled as she arranged her images on the
viewing table. There was no variety. Why hadn't
she seen that before?

Possibly because she had given the best images to Kruz?

Ronald was understandably disappointed. 'This seems to be a series of shots of the waiting staff,' he said, raising his head to pin her with a questioning stare.

'They had the most interesting faces.'

'I hope our readers agree,' Ronald said wearily, returning to studying the images Romy had set out for him. 'It seems to me you've creamed off the best shots for yourself, and that's not like you, Romy.'

A rising sense of dread hit her as Ronald removed his glasses to pinch the bridge of his nose. She needed this job. She needed the financial security and she hated letting Ronald down.

'I can't believe,' he began, 'that I send you to Argentina and you return with nothing more than half a dozen shots I can use—and not one of them of the newly married couple in the bridal suite.'

Romy huffed with frustration. Ronald really had gone too far this time. 'What did you expect? Was I supposed to swing in through their window on a vine?'

'You do whatever it takes,' he insisted. 'You do what you're famous for, Romy.'

Intruding where she wasn't wanted? Was that to be her mark on history?

'It was you who assured me you had an in to this wedding,' Ronald went on. 'When *ROCK!* was refused representation at the ceremony I felt confident that you would capture something special for us. I can't believe you've let us down. I wouldn't have given you time off for this adventure if I had known you would return with precisely nothing. You're not freelance yet, Romy,' he said, echoing her own troubled thoughts. 'But the way you're heading you'll be freelancing sooner than you want to be.'

She was only as good as her last assignment, and Ronald wouldn't forget this. She had to try and make things right. 'I must have missed something,' she said, her brain racing to find a solution. 'Let me go back and check my computer again—'

'I think you better had,' Ronald agreed. 'But not now. You look all in.'

Sympathy from Ronald was the last thing she had expected and guilty tears stung her eyes. She didn't deserve Ronald's concern. 'You're right,' she said, pulling herself together. 'Jet-lag has wiped me out. I should have waited until tomorrow. I'm sorry I've wasted your time.'

'You haven't wasted my time,' Ronald insisted. 'You just haven't shown me anything commercial— anything I can use.'

'I'm confident I can get hold of some more shots. Just give me chance to look. I don't want to disappoint you.'

'It would be the first time that you have,' Romy's

editor pointed out. 'But first I want you to promise
that you'll leave early today and try to get some rest.'

'I will,' she said, feeling worse than ever when
she saw the expression on Ronald's face.

Actually, she did feel a bit under the weather. And
to put the cap on her day she had grown a nice crop
of spots. 'I won't let you down,' she said, turning
at the door.

'Oh, I almost forgot,' Ronald said, glancing up
from the viewing table. 'There's someone waiting
for you in your office.'

Some hopeful intern, Romy guessed, no doubt
waiting in breathless anticipation for a few words
of encouragement from the once notorious and
now about to be sacked Romy Winner. She pinned
a smile to her face. No matter that she felt like a
wrung-out rag and her only specialism today was
projecting misery and failure, she would find those
words of encouragement whatever it took.

Hurrying along the corridors of power on the fifth
floor, she headed for the elevators and her lowly
cupboard in the basement. She could spare Ronald
some shots from Grace's folder. Crisis averted. She
just had to sort them out. She should have sorted
them out long before now.

But she hadn't because her head was full of Kruz.

'Thank you,' she muttered as her inner voice
stated the obvious. Actually, the real reason was
because she was still jet-lagged. She hadn't trav-

elled home in a luxurious private jet but in cattle class, with her knees on her chin in an aging commercial plane.

And whose fault was that?

'Oh, shut up,' Romy said out loud, to the consternation of her fellow travellers in the elevator.

The steel doors slid open on a different world. Gone were the cutting edge bleached oak floors of the executive level, the pale ecru paint, the state-of-the-art lighting specifically designed to draw attention to the carefully hung covers of *ROCK!* In the place of artwork, on this lowly, worker bee level was a spaghetti tangle of exposed pipework that had nothing to do with minimalist design and everything to do with neglect. A narrow avenue of peeling paint, graffiti and lino led to the door of her trash tip of a cupboard.

Stop! Breathe deeply. Pin smile to face. Open door to greet lowly, hopeful intern—

Or not!

'Language, Romy,' Kruz cautioned.

Had she said a bad word? Had she even spoken? 'Sorry,' she said with an awkward gesture. 'I'm just surprised to see you.' *To put it mildly.*

It took her a moment to rejig her thoughts. She had been wearing her most encouraging smile, anticipating an intern waiting eagerly where she had once stood, hoping for a word of encouragement to send her on her way. Romy had been lucky enough to get that word, and had been determined that whoever wanted to see her today would receive some encouragement too. She doubted Kruz needed any.

So forget the encouraging word.

Okay, then.

Standing by the chipped and shabby table that passed for her desk, Kruz Acosta, in all his business-suited magnificence, accessorised with a stone-faced stare and an over-abundance of muscle, was toying with some discarded images she had printed out, scrunched up and had been meaning to toss.

They were all of him.

CHAPTER FIVE

OKAY, SHE COULD handle this. She had to handle this. Whatever Kruz was here for *it wasn't her*.

She had to make sure he didn't leave with the impression that he had intimidated her.

And how was she going to achieve that with her heart racing off the scale?

She was going to remain calm, hold her head up high and meet him on equal ground.

'I like your office, Romy,' he murmured, in the sexy, faintly mocking voice she remembered only too well. 'Do all the executives at *ROCK!* get quite so much space?'

'Okay, okay,' she said, closing this down before he could get started. 'So space is at a premium in the city.'

The smile crept from Kruz's mouth to his eyes, which had a corresponding effect on her own expression. That was half the trouble—it was hard to remain angry with him for long. She guessed Kruz probably had the top floor of a skyscraper to himself, with a helipad as the cherry on top.

'What can I do for you, Kruz?' she said, proud of how cool she sounded.

So many things. Which was why he'd decided to call by. His office was just around the corner. And he'd needed to…to take a look at some more photographs, he remembered, jolting his mind back into gear.

'Those shots you gave me for the charity,' he said, producing the memory stick Romy had given him back in Argentina.

'What about them?' she said.

She had backed herself into the furthest corner of the room, with the desk between them like a shield. In a room as small as this he could still reach her, but he was content just to look at her. She smelled so good, so young and fresh, and she looked great. 'The shots you gave me are fantastic,' he admitted. 'So much so I'd like to see what else you've got.'

'Oh,' she said.

Was she blinking with relief? Romy could act nonchalant all she liked, but he had a sister and he knew all about acting. He took in her working outfit—the clinging leggings, flat fur boots, the long tee—and as she approached the desk and sat down he concluded that she didn't need to try hard to look great. Romy Winner was one hell of a woman. Was she ready for him now? he wondered as she bit down on her lip.

'We've decided the charity should have a calendar,' he said, 'and we thought you could help. What you've given me so far are mostly people shots, which are great—but there are too many celebrities. And the royals… Great shots, but they're not what we need.'

'What do you want?' she said.

'Those character studies of people who've worked on the *estancia* for most of their lives. Group shots used to be taken in the old days, as well as individual portraits, and that's a tradition I'd like to revive. You make everyone look like members of the same family, which is how I've always seen it.'

'Team Acosta?' she suggested, the shadow of a smile creeping onto her lips.

'Exactly,' he agreed. He was glad he didn't have to spell it out to her. On reflection, he didn't have to spell anything out for Romy. She *got* him.

'What about scenery, wildlife—that sort of thing?' she said, turning to her screen.

'Perfect. I think we're going to make one hell of a calendar,' he enthused as she brought up some amazing images.

Hallelujah! She could hardly believe her luck. This was incredible. She wouldn't lose her job after all. Of course a charity would want vistas and wildlife images, while Ronald wanted all the shots Kruz wanted to discard. She hadn't been thinking straight in Argentina—*for some reason*—and had loaded pictures into files without thinking things through.

'So you don't mind if I have the people shots back?' she confirmed, wondering if it was possible to overdose on Kruz's drugging scent.

'Not at all,' he said, in the low, sexy drawl that made her wish she'd bothered to put some make-up on this morning, gelled her hair and covered her spots.

'You look tired, Romy,' he added as she started loading images onto a clean memory stick. 'You don't have to do this now. I can come back later.'

'Better you stay so you're sure you get what you want,' she said.

'Okay, I will,' he said, hiding his wry smile. 'Thanks for doing this at such short notice.'

She couldn't deny she was puzzled. He was happy to stay? Either Kruz wanted this calendar really badly, or he was…what? Checking up on her? Checking her out?

Not the latter, Romy concluded. Kruz could have anyone he wanted, and London was chock-a-block full of beautiful women. Hard luck for her, when she still wanted him and felt connected to him in a way she couldn't explain.

Fact: what happened in the press coach is history. Get used to it.

With a sigh she lifted her shoulders and dropped

them again in response to her oh, so sensible inner voice. Wiping a hand across her forehead, she wondered if it was hot in here.

'Are you okay?' Kruz asked with concern.

No. She felt faint. Another first. 'Of course,' she said brightly, getting back to her work.

The tiny room was buzzing with Kruz's energy, she thought—which was the only reason her head was spinning. She stopped to take a swig of water from the plastic bottle on her desk, but she still didn't feel that great.

'Will you excuse me for a moment?' she said shakily, blundering to her feet.

She didn't wait to hear Kruz's answer. Rushing from the desk, she just made it to the rest room in time to be heartily sick.

It was just a reaction at having her underground bunker invaded by Kruz Acosta, Romy reasoned as she studied the green sheen on her face. Swilling her face with cold water, she took a drink and several deep breaths before heading back to her room— and she only did that when she was absolutely certain that the brief moment of weakness had been and gone.

He was worried about Romy. She looked pale.

'No... No, I'm fine,' she said when he asked her if she was all right as she breezed back into the room. 'Must have been something I ate. Sorry. You don't need to hear that.'

He shrugged. 'I was brought up on a farm. I'm not as rarefied as you seem to think.'

'Not rarefied at all,' she said, flashing him a glance that jolted him back to a grassy bank and a blue-black sky.

'It's hot in here,' he observed. No wonder she felt faint. Opening the door, he stuck a chair in the way. Not that it did much good. The basement air was stale. He hated the claustrophobic surroundings.

'Why don't you sit and relax while I do this?' she suggested, without turning from the screen.

'It won't take long, will it?'

She shook her head.

'Then I'll stand, thank you.'

In the tiny room that meant he was standing close behind her. He was close enough to watch Romy's neck flush as pink as her cheeks.

With arousal? With awareness of him?

He doubted it was a response to the images she was bringing up on the screen.

He felt a matching surge of interest. Even under the harsh strip-light Romy's skin looked as temptingly soft as a peach. And her birdwing-black hair, which she hadn't bothered to gel today, was enticingly thick and silky. A cluster of fat, glossy curls caressed her neck and softened her un-made-up face...

She was lovely.

She felt better, so there was no reason for this

raised heartbeat apart from Kruz. Normally she could lose herself in work, but not today. He was such a presence in the small, dingy room—such a presence in her life. Shaking her head, she gave a wry smile.

'Is something amusing you?' he said.

'No,' she said, leaning closer to the screen, as if the answer to her amusement lay there. There was nothing amusing about her thoughts. She should be ashamed, not smiling asininely as it occurred to her that she had never seen Kruz close up in the light other than through her camera. Of course she knew to her cost that close up he was an incredible force. She was feeling something of that now. She could liken it to being close to a soft-pawed predator, never being quite sure when it would pounce and some-how—insanely—longing for that moment.

'There. All done,' she said in a brisk tone, swinging round to face him.

It was a shock to find him staring at her as if his thoughts hadn't all been of business. Confusion flooded her. Confusion wasn't something she was familiar with—except when Kruz was around. The expression in his eyes didn't help her to regain her composure. Kruz had the most incredible eyes. They were dark and compelling, and he had the longest eyelashes she'd ever seen.

'These are excellent,' he said, distracting her.

'When you've copied them to a memory stick you'll keep copies on your computer, I presume?'

'Yes, of course,' she said, struggling to put her mind in gear and match him with her business plan going forward. 'They're all in a file, so if you want more, or you lose them, just ask me.' *For anything,* she thought.

'And you can supply whatever I need?'

She hesitated before answering, and turning back to the screen flicked through the images one more time. 'Are you pleased?'

'I'm very pleased,' Kruz confirmed.

Even now he'd pulled back he couldn't get that far away, and he was close enough to make her ears tingle. She kept her gaze on the monitor, not trusting herself to look round. This was not Romy Winner, thick-skinned photojournalist, but someone who felt as self-conscious as a teenager on her first date. But she wasn't a kid, and this wasn't a date. This was the man she'd had sex with after knowing him for around half an hour. When thousands of miles divided them she could just about live with that, but when Kruz was here in her office—

'Your compositions are really good, Romy.'

She exhaled shakily, wondering if it was only she who could feel the electricity between them.

'These shots are perfect for the calendar,' he went on, apparently immune to all the things she was feeling.

She logged off, wanting him to go now, so her wounded heart would get half a chance to heal.

'And on behalf of the family,' Kruz was saying. 'I'm asking you to handle this project for us.'

She swung round. Wiping a hand across her face, she wondered what she'd missed.

'That's if you've got time?' Kruz said, seeming faintly amused as he stared down at her. 'And don't worry—my office is just around the corner, so I'll be your liaison in London.'

Don't worry?

Her heart was thundering as he went on.

'I'd like to see a mock-up of the calendar when you've completed it. I don't foresee any problems, just so long as you remember that quality is all-important when it comes to the Acosta charity.'

Her head was reeling. Was she hearing straight? The Acosta family was giving her the break she had longed for? She couldn't think straight for all the emotion bursting inside her. She had to concentrate really hard to take in everything Kruz was telling her. A commission for the Acosta family? What better start could she have?

Something that didn't potentially tie her in to Kruz?

She mustn't think about that now. She just had to say yes before she lost it completely.

'No,' she blurted, as the consequences of seeing

Kruz again and again and again sank in. 'I'd love to do it, but—'

'But what?' he said with surprise.

Answering his question meant looking into that amazing face. And she could do that. But to keep on seeing Kruz day after day, knowing she meant nothing to him... That would be too demoralising even to contemplate. 'I'd love to do it,' she said honestly, feeling her spirit sag as she began to destroy her chances of doing so, 'but I don't have time. I'm really sorry, Kruz, but I'm just too tied up here—'

'Enjoying the security that comes with working for one of the top magazines?' he interrupted, glancing round. 'I can see it would take guts to take time out from *this*.'

She wasn't in the mood for his mockery.

'No worries,' he said, smiling faintly as he moved towards the door. 'I'll just tell Grace you can't find the time to do it.'

'Grace?' she said.

'Grace is our new patron. It was Grace who suggested I approach you—but I'm sure there are plenty of other photographers who can do the job.'

Ouch!

'Wait—'

Kruz paused with his hand on the door. She remembered those hands from the grassy bank and from the press coach, and she remembered what they were capable of. Shivering with longing, she folded her arms around her waist and hugged herself tight.

'Well?' Kruz prompted. 'What am I going to say to Grace? Do you have a message for her, Romy?'

How could she let Grace down? Grace was trying to help her. They had had a long talk when Romy had first arrived in Argentina. Grace had been so easy to talk to that Romy had found herself pouring out her hopes and dreams for the future. She had never done that with anyone before, but somehow her words came easily when she was with Grace. Maybe Grace's gentle nature had allowed her to lower her guard for once.

'I'll do it,' she said quietly.

'Good,' Kruz confirmed, as if he had known she would all along.

She should be imagining her relief when he closed the door behind him rather than wishing he would stay so they could discuss this some more—so she could keep him here until they shared more than just memories of hot sex on someone else's wedding day.

'Romy? You don't seem as pleased about this work as I expected you to be.'

She flushed as Kruz's gaze skimmed over her body. 'Of course I'm pleased.'

'So I can tell Grace you'll do this for her?'

'I'd rather tell her myself.'

Kruz's powerful shoulders eased in a shrug. 'As you wish.'

There was still nothing for her on that stony face, but she was hardly known for shows of emotion herself. Like Kruz, she preferred to be the one in control. A further idea chilled her as they locked stares. Romy's control came from childhood, when showing emotion would only have made things worse for her mother. When her father was in one of his rages she'd just had to wait quietly until he was out of the way before she could go to look after her mother, or he'd go for her too, and then she'd be in no state to help. Control was just as important to Kruz, which prompted the question: what dark secret was he hiding?

Romy worked off her passions at the gym in the kick-boxing ring, where she found the discipline integral to martial arts steadying. Maybe Kruz found the same. His instinctive and measured response to her roundhouse kick pointed to someone for whom keeping his feelings in check was a way of life.

The only time she had lost it was in Argentina, Romy reflected, when something inside her had snapped. *The Kruz effect?* All those years of training and learning how to govern her emotions had been lost in one passionate encounter.

She covered this disturbing thought with the blandest of questions. 'Is that everything?'

'For now.'

Ice meets ice—today. In Argentina they had been on fire for each other. But theirs was a business relationship now, Romy reminded herself as Kruz prepared to leave. She had to stop thinking about being crushed against his hard body, the minty taste of his sexy mouth, or the sweet, nagging ache that had decided to lodge itself for the duration of his visit at the apex of her thighs. If he knew about that she'd be in real trouble.

'It's been good to see you again,' she said, as if to test her conviction that she was capable of keeping up this cool act.

'Romy,' Kruz said, acknowledging her with a dip of his head and just the slightest glint of humour in his eyes.

The Acosta brothers weren't exactly known for being monks. Kruz was simply being polite and friendly. 'It will be good to be in regular contact with Grace,' she said, moving off her chair to show him out.

'Talking of which…' He paused outside her door.

'Yes?' She tried to appear nonchalant, but she felt faint again.

'We're holding a benefit on Saturday night for the charity, at one of the London hotels. Grace will be there, and I thought it would be a great opportunity for you two to get together and for you to meet my family so you can understand what the charity means to us. That's if you're interested?' he said wryly.

She stared into Kruz's eyes, trying to work out

his motive for asking her. Was it purely business, or something else…?

His weary sigh jolted her back to the present. 'When you're ready?' he prompted, staring pointedly at his watch.

'Saturday…?'

'Yes or no?'

He said it with about as much enthusiasm as if he were booking the local plumber to sort out a blocked drain. 'Thank you,' she said formally. 'As you say, it's too good a chance to miss—seeing Grace and the rest of your family.'

'I'm glad to hear it. There may be more work coming your way if the calendar is a success. A newsletter, for example.'

'That's a great idea. Shall I bring my camera?'

'Leave it behind this time,' Kruz suggested, his dark glance flickering over her as he named the hotel where they were to meet.

She couldn't pretend not to be impressed.

'Dress up,' he said.

She gave him a look that said no one told her what to wear. But on this occasion it wasn't about her. This was for Grace. She still felt a bit mulish—if only because Kruz was the type of man she guessed liked his women served up fancy, with all the trimmings. Elusive as he was, she'd seen a couple of shots of him with society beauties, and though he had looked bored on each occasion the girls had been immaculately groomed. But, in fairness to the women, the only time she'd seen Kruz animated was in the throes of passion.

'Something funny?' he said.

'I'll wear my best party dress,' she promised him with a straight face.

'Saturday,' he said, straightening up to his full imposing height. 'I'll pick you up your place at eight.'

Her eyes widened. She had thought he'd meet her at the hotel. Was she Kruz's *date*?

No, stupid. He's just making sure you don't change your mind and let The Family down.

'That's fine by me,' she confirmed. 'Before you go I'll jot my address down for you.'

He almost cracked a smile. 'Have you forgotten what business I'm in?'

Okay, Señor Control-Freak-Security-Supremo. Point taken.

Her address was no secret anyway, Romy reasoned, telling herself to calm down. 'Eight o' clock,' she said, holding Kruz's mocking stare in a steady beam.

'Until Saturday, Romy.'

'Kruz.'

She only realised when she'd closed the door behind him and her legs almost gave way that she was shaking. Leaning back against the peeling paintwork, she waited until Kruz's footsteps had died away and there was nothing to disrupt the silence apart from the hum of the fluorescent light.

This was ridiculous, she told herself some time later. She was being everything she had sworn never to be. She had allowed herself to become a victim of her own overstretched heart.

There was only one cure for this, Romy decided, and she would find it when she worked out her frustrations in the ring at the gym tonight. Meanwhile she would lose herself in work. Maybe tonight she would be better giving the punch-bag a workout rather than taking on a sparring partner. She didn't trust herself with a living, breathing opponent in her present mood. And she needed the gym. She needed to rebalance her confidence levels before Saturday. She wanted to feel her strength and rejoice in it—her strength of will, in particular. She had to remember that she was strong and successful and independent and safe—and she planned to keep it that way. She especially had to remember that on Saturday.

Saturday!

What the hell was she going to wear?

CHAPTER SIX

'LOOKING HOT,' ONE of the guys said in passing, throwing a wry smile her way as Romy finished her final set of blows on the punch-bag.

The bag must have taken worse in its time, but it had surely never taken a longer or more fearsomely sustained attack from a small angry woman with more frustration to burn off than she could handle. Romy nodded her head in acknowledgement of the praise. This gym wasn't a place for designer-clad bunnies to scope each other out. This was a serious working gym, where many of the individuals went on to have successful careers in their chosen sport.

'What's eating you, Romy?' demanded the grizzled old coach who ran the place, showing more insight into Romy's bruised and battered psyche than her fellow athlete as Romy rested, panting, with her still gloved hands braced on her knees. 'Man trouble?'

You know me too well, she thought, though she denied it. 'You know me, Charlie,' she said, straightening up. 'Have camera, will travel. No man gets in the way of that.'

'I bet that camera's cosy to snuggle up to on a cold night,' Charlie murmured in an undertone as he moved on to oversee the action in another part of his kingdom.

What did Charlie know? What did *anyone* know? Romy scowled as she caught sight of herself in one of the gym's full-length mirrors. What man in his right mind would want a sweating firebrand with more energy than sense? *Kruz wouldn't.* With her bandaged hands, bitten nails, boy's shorts and clinging, unflattering vest, she looked about as appealing as a wet Sunday. She probably smelled great too. Taking a step back, she nodded her thanks as another athlete offered to help her with the gloves.

'Looking fierce,' he said.

'Ain't that the truth?' Romy murmured. She was a proper princess, complete with grubby sweatband holding her electro-static hair off her surly, sweaty face.

He saw her the moment he walked into the gym. Or rather something drew his stare to her. She felt him too. Even with her back turned he saw a quiver of awareness ripple down her spine. And now she was swinging slowly round, as if she had to confirm her hunch was correct.

We have to stop meeting like this, he thought as

they stared at each other. He nodded curtly. Romy nodded back. Yet again rather than looking at him, like other women, Romy Winner was staring at him as if she was trying to psych him out before they entered the ring.

That could be arranged too, he reflected.

They were still giving each other the hard stare when the elderly owner of the gym came up to him. 'Hey, Charlie.' He turned, throwing his towel round his neck so he could extend a hand to greet an old friend warmly.

'You've spotted our lady champion, I see,' Charlie commented.

Kruz turned back to stare at Romy. 'I've seen her.'

Romy had finished her routine. He was about to start his. She looked terrific. It would be rude not to speak to her.

Oh... Argh! What the...?

Romy blenched. For goodness' sake, how could anyone look *that* good? Kruz was ridiculously handsome. And what the hell was he doing in *her* gym? Wasn't there somewhere billionaire health freaks could hang out together and leave lesser mortals alone to feel good about themselves a few times a week?

Even with the unforgiving lights of the workmanlike sports hall blazing down on him Kruz looked hot. Tall, tanned and broader than the other men sharing his space, he drew attention like nothing else. And he was coming over—oh, *good*. Even a warrior woman needed to shower occasionally, and Kruz was as fresh as a daisy.

Gym kit suited him, she decided as he advanced. With his confident stroll and those scars and tattoos showing beneath his skimpy top he was a fine sight. She wanted him all over again. If she'd never met him before she'd want him. And, inconveniently, she wanted him twice as much as she ever had. A quick glance around reassured Romy that she wasn't the only one staring. She couldn't blame the gym members for that. Muscles bunched beneath his ripped and faded top, and the casual training pants hung off his hips. Silently, she whimpered.

And Kruz didn't walk, he prowled, Romy reflected, holding her ground as he closed the distance between them. His pace was unhurried but remorseless and, brave as she was, she felt her throat dry—it was about the only part of her that was.

'We meet again,' he said with some amusement, stopping tantalisingly within touching distance.

'I didn't expect it to be so soon,' she said off-handedly, reaching for a towel just as someone else picked it up.

'Here—have this. I can always grab another.'

'I couldn't possibly—'

Kruz tossed his towel around her neck. Taking

the edges, she wrapped it round her shoulders like a cloak. It still held his warmth.

'So you're really serious about the gym?' he said.

'I like to break sweat,' she agreed, shooting him a level stare as if daring him to find fault with that. 'Why haven't I seen you here before?' she said as an afterthought. 'You slumming it?'

'Please,' Kruz murmured. 'My office is only round the corner.'

'And you don't have a gym?' she said, opening her eyes wide with mock surprise.

'It's under construction,' he said, giving her the cynical look he was so good at.

'I'm impressed,' she said.

'You should be.'

If only that crease in his cheek wasn't so attractive. 'Maybe I'll come and take a look at it when it's finished.'

'I might hold you to that.'

Please. 'I'm very busy,' she said dryly, still holding the dark, compelling stare. 'I have a very demanding private client.'

Kruz's eyes narrowed as he held her gaze. 'I hope I know him.'

'I think you do. So, how do you know Charlie?' she said, seizing on the first thing that came to mind to break the stare-off between them.

'Charlie's an old friend,' Kruz explained, pulling back.

'Were you both in the army?' she asked on a hunch.

'Same regiment,' Kruz confirmed, but then he went quiet and the smile died in his eyes. 'I'd better get started,' he said.

'And I'd better go take my shower,' she agreed as they parted.

'Don't miss the fun,' Charlie called after her.

'What fun?'

'Don't miss Kruz in the ring.'

She turned to look at him.

'Why don't you come in the ring with me?' Kruz suggested. 'You could be my second.'

'Sorry. I don't do second.'

He laughed. 'Or you could fight me,' he suggested.

'Do I look stupid? Don't answer that,' she said quickly, holding up her hands as Kruz shot her a look.

This was actually turning out better than she had thought when she'd first seen Kruz walk into the gym. They were sparring in good way—verbally teasing each other—and she liked that. It made her feel warm inside.

Charlie caught up with her on the way to the changing rooms. 'Don't be too hard on him, Romy.'

'Who are we talking about? Kruz?'

'You know who we're talking about,' the old pro said, glancing around to make sure they weren't being overheard. 'Believe me, Romy, you have no idea what that man's been through.'

'No, I don't,' she agreed. 'I don't know anything about him. Why would I?'

Did Charlie know anything? Had Kruz said something? Her antennae were twitching on full alert.

'You should know what he's done for his friends,' Charlie went on, speaking out of the corner of his mouth. 'The lives he's saved—the things he's seen.'

The guarded expression left her face. This was the longest speech she had ever heard Charlie make. There was no doubt in her mind Charlie was sincere, and she felt reassured that Kruz hadn't said anything about their encounter to him. 'I don't think Kruz wants anyone to go easy on him,' she said thoughtfully, 'but I'll certainly bear in mind what you've said.'

Charlie shook his head in mock disapproval. 'You're a hard woman, Romy Winner. You two deserve each other.'

'Now, that's something I have to disagree with,' Romy said, lightening up. 'You just don't know your clientele, Charlie. Shame on you.' She smiled as she gave Charlie a wink.

'I know them better than you think,' Charlie muttered beneath his breath as Romy shouldered her way into the women's changing room. 'Go take that shower, then join me ringside,' he called after her.

Romy rushed through her shower, emptying a

whole bottle of shower gel over her glowing body before lathering her hair with a half a bottle of shampoo. The white tiled floor in the utilitarian shower block was like a skating rink by the time she had finished. Thank goodness her hair was short, she reflected, frantically towelling down. She didn't want to miss a second of this bout. She stared at herself in the mirror. Make-up? Her eyes were bright enough with excitement and her cheeks were flushed. Tugging on her leggings, her flat boots and grey hoodie, she swung her gym bag on to her shoulder and went to join the crowd assembling around the ring at the far end of the gym.

The scent of clean sweat mingled with anticipation came to greet her. This was her sort of party.

'Quite a crowd,' she remarked to Charlie, feeling her heart lurch as Kruz vaulted the ropes into the ring. When he turned to look at her, her heart went crazy. Naked to the waist, Kruz was so hot her body couldn't wait to remind her about getting up close and personal with him. She pressed her thighs together, willing the feeling to subside. No such luck. As Kruz turned his back and she saw his muscles flex the pulse only grew stronger.

'It's not often we get two champions in the ring— even here at my gym,' Charlie said, his scratchy voice tense with anticipation.

The other kick-boxer was a visitor from the north of England called Heath Stamp. He'd been a bad boy too, according to rumour, and Romy knew him by reputation as a formidable fighter. But Heath was nothing compared to Kruz in her eyes. Kruz's hard, bronzed body gleamed with energy beneath the lights. He was a man in the peak of health, just approaching his prime.

A man with the potential to happily service a harem of women.

'Stop,' she said out loud, in the hope of silencing her inner voice.

'Did you say something, Romy?' Charlie enquired politely, cupping his ear.

'No—just a reminder to myself,' she said dryly.

'There's no one else the champ can spar with,' Charlie confided, without allowing his attention to be deflected for a second from the ring.

'Lucky Kruz came along, then.'

'I'm talking about Kruz,' Charlie rebuked her. 'Kruz is the champ. I should know. I trained him in the army.'

She turned to stare at the rapt face of the elderly man standing next to her. He knew more about Kruz than she did. And he would be reluctant to part with a single shred of information unless it was general info like Kruz's exploits in the gym. What *was* it with Charlie today? She'd never seen him so animated. She'd never seen such fierce loyalty in his eyes or heard it in his voice. It made her want to know all those things Kruz kept secret—for he did keep secrets. Of that much she was certain.

So some men were as complex as women, Romy reasoned, telling herself not to make a big deal out of it as the referee brought the two combatants together in the centre of the ring. Kruz was entitled to his privacy as much as she was, and he was lucky to have a loyal friend like Charlie.

As the bout got under way and the onlookers started cheering Romy only had eyes for one man. The skill level was intense, but there was something about Kruz that transcended skill and made him a master. Being a fighter herself, she suspected that he was holding back. She wondered about this, knowing Kruz could have ended the match in Round One if he had wanted to. Instead he chose to see it through until his opponent began to flag, when Kruz called a halt. Proclaiming the match a draw, he bumped the glove of his opponent, raising Heath Stamp's arm high in the air before the referee could say a word about it.

'That's one of the benefits of having a special attachment to this gym,' Kruz explained, laughing when she pulled him up on it as he vaulted the ropes to land at her side.

'A special attachment?' she probed.

'I used to own it,' he revealed casually, his voice muffled as he rubbed his face on a towel.

'You used to own this gym?'

'That's right,' Kruz confirmed, pulling the towel down.

She glanced round, frowning. Charlie was busy consoling the other fighter. She'd known Charlie for a number of years and had always assumed *he* owned the gym. 'I had no idea you were in the leisure industry,' she said, turning back to Kruz.

'Amongst other things.' Grabbing a water bottle from his second, Kruz drank deeply before pouring the rest over his head. 'I own a lot of gyms, Romy.'

'News to me.'

'My apologies,' he said with a wry look. 'I'll make sure my PA puts you on my "needs to know" list right away.'

'See that you do,' she said, with a mock-fierce stare. Were they getting on? Were they *really* getting on?

'So, what are you doing next?' Kruz asked her.

'Going home.'

'What about food?'

'What about it? I'm not hungry.'

'Surely you're over your sickness now?'

'Yes, of course I am.' Actually, she *had* felt queasy again earlier on.

'Hang on while I take a shower,' he said. 'I'll see you in Reception in ten.'

'But—'

That was all she had time for before Kruz headed

off. Raking her short hair with frustration, she was left to watch him run the gauntlet of admirers on his way to the men's changing room. Why did he want to eat with her? Or was food not on the menu? Her heart lurched alarmingly at the thought that it might not be. She wasn't about to fall into ever-ready mode. Just because she enjoyed sex with a certain man it did *not* mean Kruz had a supply on tap.

In all probability he just wanted to talk about the charity project, her sensible self reassured her.

And if he didn't want to chat...?

They'd be in a café somewhere. What was the worst that could happen?

They'd leave the food and run?

Clearly the bout had put Kruz in a good mood, Romy concluded as he came through the inner doors into the reception area.

'Ready to go?' he said, holding the door for her.

So far so good. Brownie points for good manners duly awarded.

'There's a place just around the corner,' he said, 'where we can get something to eat.'

'I know it.' He was referring to the café they all called the Greasy Spoon—though nothing could be further from the truth. True enough, it was a no-nonsense feeding station, with bright lights, Formica tables, hard chairs, but there was a really good cook on the grill who served up high-quality ingredients for impatient athletes with colossal appetites.

They found a table in the window. There wasn't much of a view as it was all steamed up. The air-conditioning was an open door at the back of the kitchen.

'Okay here?' Kruz said when they were settled.

'Fine. Thank you.' She refused to be overawed by him—but that wasn't easy when her mind insisted on undressing him.

She was working for the Acosta family now, Romy reminded herself, and she had to concentrate on that. It was just a bit odd, having had the most amazing sex with this man and having to pretend they had not. Kruz seemed to have forgotten all about it—or maybe it was just one more appetite to slake, she reflected as the waitress came to take their order.

'Do you mind if I take a photo of you?' she said, pulling out her phone.

'Why?' Kruz said suspiciously.

'Why the phone? I don't have my camera.'

'Why the photograph?'

'Because you look half human—because this is a great setting—because everyone thinks of the Acostas as rarefied beings who live on a different planet to them. I just want to show people that you do normal things too.'

'Steak and chips?' Kruz suggested wryly, tugging off his heavy jacket.

'Steak and chips,' she agreed, returning his smile.

Oh, boy, how that smile of his heated her up. 'You'd better not be laughing at me,' she warned, running off a series of shots.

'Let me see,' he said, holding out his hand for her phone.

'Me first,' she argued. *Wow.* She blew out a slow, controlled breath as she studied the shot. Kruz's thick, slightly too long hair waved and gleamed like mahogany beneath the lights. The way it caught on his sideburns and stubble was…

'Romy?' he said

'Not yet,' she teased. 'You'll have to wait for the newsletter.' *To see those powerful shoulders clad in the softest air-force blue cashmere and those well-packed worn and faded jeans…*

'Romy?' Kruz said, sounding concerned when she went off into her own little dreamworld.

Snap! Snap!

'There. That should do it,' she said, passing the phone across the table.

'Not bad,' Kruz admitted grudgingly. 'You've reminded me I need to shave.'

'Glad to be of service,' she said, blushing furiously half a beat later. Being that type of service was not what she meant, she assured herself sternly as Kruz pushed the phone back to her side of the table.

Fortunately their food arrived, letting her off the hook. She had ordered a Caesar salad with prawn, while Kruz had ordered steak and fries. Both meals were huge. And every bit as delicious as expected.

'This is a great place,' she said, tucking in. As Kruz murmured agreement she made the mistake of glancing at his mouth. Fork suspended, she stared until she realised he was looking at her mouth too. 'Yours good?' she murmured distractedly. Kruz had a really sexy mouth. And an Olympian appetite, she registered as he called for a side of mushrooms, onion rings and a salad to add to his order.

'Something wrong with your meal, Romy?'

'No. It's delicious.' She stared intently at her salad, determined not to be distracted by him again.

Food was a great ice-breaker. It oiled the wheels of conversation better than anything she knew. 'So, tell me more about Charlie's gym. I've been going there for years and I had no idea you used to own it.'

Kruz frowned. 'What do you want to know?'

'I always thought Charlie owned it. Not that it matters,' she said.

'He does own it.' And, when she continued to urge him on with a look of interest, Kruz offered cryptically, 'Things change over time, Romy.'

'Right.' The conversation seemed to have gone the same way as their empty plates. 'Charlie never stopped talking about you,' she said to open it up again. 'He admires you so much, Kruz.'

Personal comments were definitely a no-no, she concluded as Kruz gave her a flat black look. 'Do you want coffee?' He was already reaching for his wallet. This down-time was over.

'No. I'm fine. Let me get this.'

For once in her life she managed not to fumble and got out a couple of twenties to hand to the waitress before Kruz had a chance to disagree.

He did not look pleased. 'You should not have done that,' he said.

'Why not? Because you're rich and I'm not?'

'Don't be so touchy, Romy.'

She was touchy? 'I'm not touchy,' she protested, standing up. 'Aren't you the guy who's taking me to some swish event on Saturday?' She shrugged. 'The least I can do is buy you dinner.'

'You will be a guest of the family on Saturday,' he said.

Heaven forfend she should mistake it for a date.

'And where Charlie's concerned I'd prefer you don't say anything about the gym to him,' Kruz added. 'That man is not and never has been in my debt. If anything, I'm in his.'

She hadn't anticipated such a speech, and wondered what lay behind it—especially in light of Charlie's words about Kruz. *The plot thickens,* she thought. But as it showed no sign of being solved any time soon she followed Kruz to the door.

'Until Saturday,' he said, barely turning to look at her as he spoke.

Someone was touchy when it came to questions

about his past. 'I'll meet you at the hotel,' she said briskly, deciding she really did not want him at her place. She was surprised when he didn't argue.

She watched Kruz thread his way through the congested traffic with easy grace—talking of which, for Grace's sake she would find something other than sweats or leggings to wear on Saturday night. She wanted to do the family proud. She didn't want to stand out for all the wrong reasons. Khalifa's department store was on her way home, so she had no excuse.

In the sale she picked out an understated column of deep blue silk that came somewhere just above her knees. It was quite flattering. The rich blue made her hair seem shinier and brought out the colour of her eyes. No gel or red tips on Saturday, she thought, viewing herself in the mirror. She normally dressed to please herself, but she didn't want to let Grace down. And, okay, maybe she *did* want strut her stuff just a little bit in front of Kruz. This was one occasion when being 'wiry', as Charlie frequently and so unflatteringly referred to her, was actually an advantage. The sale stuff was all in tiny sizes. She even tried on a pair of killer heels—samples, the salesgirl told her.

'That's why they're in the sale,' the girl explained. 'You're the first person who can get her feet into them. They're size Tinkerbell.'

Romy slanted her a smile. 'Tinkerbell suits me fine. I always did like to create a bit of mayhem.'

They both laughed as they took Romy's haul to the till.

'You'll have men flocking,' the girl told her as she rang up Romy's purchases.

'Yeah, right.' And the one man she would like to come flocking would be totally unmoved. 'Thanks for all your help,' Romy said, flashing a goodbye smile as she picked up the bag.

CHAPTER SEVEN

SOMETHING PROPELLED HIM to his feet. Romy had just entered the sumptuously dressed ballroom. He might have known. Animal instinct had driven him to his feet, he acknowledged wryly as that same instinct transferred to his groin. Romy had taken his hint to dress for the occasion, expanding his thoughts as to what she might wear beyond his wildest dreams. Hunger pounded in his eyes as her slanting navy blue gaze found his. Nothing could have prepared him for this level of transformation, or for the way she made him feel. He acted nonchalant as she began to weave her way through the other guests, heading for their table, but with that short blue-black hair, elfin face and the understated silk dress she was easily the most desirable woman in the room.

'Kruz...'

'Romy,' he murmured as she drew to a halt in front of him.

'Allow me introduce you around,' he said, eventually remembering his manners.

His family smiled at Romy and then glanced at him. He was careful to remain stonily impassive. His PA had arranged the place cards so that Romy was seated on the opposite side of the table to him, where he could observe her without the need to engage her in conversation. He had thought he would prefer it that way, but when he saw the way his hot-blooded brothers reacted to her he wasn't so sure.

It was only when it came to the pudding course and Grace suggested they should all change places that he could breathe easily again.

'So,' he said, settling down in the chair next to Romy, 'what did you and Grace decide about the charity?' The two women hadn't stopped talking all evening and had made an arresting sight, Grace with her refined blond beauty and Romy the cute little gamine at her side.

'We discussed the possibility of a regular newsletter, with lots of photographs to show what we do.'

'We?' he queried.

'Do you want me to own this or not?' Romy parried with a shrewd stare.

'Of course I do. It's important to me that everyone involved feels fully committed to the project.' Surprisingly, he found Romy's business persona incredibly sexy. 'That's how I've found employees like it in the past.'

'I'm not your employee. I work for myself, Kruz.'

'Of course you do,' he said, holding her gaze until her cheeks pinked up.

She was all business now—talking about anything but personal matters. That was what he expected of Romy in this new guise, but it didn't mean he had to like it.

'We also talked about a range of greetings cards to complement the calendar—Kruz, are you listening to me?'

'It sounds as if you and Grace have made a good start,' he said, leaning back in his chair.

The urge to sit with Romy and monopolise her conversation wasn't so much a case of being polite as a hunting imperative. His brothers were still sitting annoyingly close to her, though in fairness she didn't seem to notice them.

She was so aroused she was finding it embarrassing. Her cheeks were flushed and she didn't even dare to look down to see if her ever-ready nipples were trying to thrust their way through the flimsy silk. She couldn't breathe properly while she was sitting this close to Kruz—she couldn't think. She could only feel. And there was a lot of feeling going on. Her lips felt full, her eyes felt sultry. Her breasts felt heavy. And her nipples were outrageously erect. *There*. She knew she shouldn't have looked. Her breathing was super-fast, and she felt swollen and needy and—

'More wine, madam?'

'No, thank you,' she managed to squeak out. She'd hardly touched the first glass. Who needed stimulus when Kruz Acosta was sitting next to her?

'Would you like to dance?'

She gaped at the question and Kruz raised a brow.

'It's quite a simple question,' he pointed out, 'and all you have to say is yes or no.'

For once in her life she couldn't say anything at all. The table was emptying around them. Everyone was on their feet, dirty-dancing to a heady South American beat. The dance floor was packed. Kruz was only being polite, she reasoned. And she could hardly refuse him without appearing rude.

'Okay,' she said, trying for off-hand as she left the table.

There was only one problem here—her legs felt like jelly and sensation had gathered where it shouldn't, rivalling the music with a compelling pulse. Worse, Kruz was staring knowingly into her eyes. He didn't need to say a word. She was already remembering a grassy bank beneath a night sky in Argentina and a press coach rocking. His touch on her back was all the more frustrating for being light. They had around six inches of dance floor to play in and Kruz seemed determined they would use only half those inches. Pressed up hard against him, she was left wondering if she could lose control right here, right now. The way sensation was mounting inside her made that seem not only possible but extremely probable.

'Are you all right, Romy?' Kruz asked.

She heard the strand of amusement in his voice. He knew, damn him! 'Depends what you mean by all right?' she said.

Somehow she managed to get through the rest of the dance without incident, and neither of them spoke a word on their way back to the table. The palm of Kruz's hand felt warm on her back, and maybe that soothed her into a dream state, for the next thing she knew he had led her on past the table, through the exit and on towards the elevators.

They stood without explanation, movement or speech as the small, luxuriously upholstered cabin rose swiftly towards one of the higher floors. She didn't mean to stare at it, but there was a cosy-looking banquette built into one side of the restricted space. She guessed it was a thoughtful gesture by the hotel for some of its older guests. Generously padded and upholstered in crimson velvet, the banquette was exerting a strangely hypnotic effect on her—that and the mirror on the opposite side.

She sucked in a swift, shocked breath as Kruz stopped the elevator between floors.

'No...' she breathed.

'Too much of a cliché?' he suggested, with that wicked grin she loved curving his mouth.

They came together like a force of nature. It took

all he'd got to hold Romy off long enough for him to protect them both. Remembering the last time, when she had wrenched the shirt from his pants, he kept her hands pinned above her head as he kissed her, pressing her hard against the wall. She tasted fresh and clean and young and perfect—all the things he was not. His stubble scraped her as he buried his face in her neck and her lips were already bruised. Inhaling deeply, he kissed her below the ear for the sheer pleasure of feeling tremors course through her body. His hands moved quickly to cup the sweet remembered swell of her buttocks.

This was everything he remembered, only better. Her skin was silky-smooth. His rough hands were full of her. In spite of being so tiny she had curves in all the right places and she fitted him perfectly. Lodging one thigh between her legs, he moved her dress up to her waist and brought her lacy underwear down. 'Wrap your legs around me, Romy,' he ordered, positioning her on the very edge of the banquette.

Pressing her knees back, he stared down as he tested that she was ready. This was the first time he had seen her—really seen her—and she was more than ready. Those tremors had travelled due south and were gripping her insistently now.

'Oh, please,' she gasped, holding her thighs wide for him.

She alternated her pleas to him with glances in the

mirror, where he knew the sight of him ready and more than willing to do what both of them needed so badly really turned her on. He obliged by running the tip of his straining erection against her. She panted and mewled as she tried to thrust her hips towards him to capture more. He had her in a firm grasp, and though he was equally hungry it pleased him to make her wait.

'What do you want?' he murmured against her mouth, teasing her with his tongue.

He should have known Romy Winner would tell him, in no uncertain language. With a laugh he sank deep, and rested a moment while she uttered a series of panting cries.

'Good?' he enquired softly.

Her answer was to groan as she threw her head back. Withdrawing slowly, he sank again—slowly and to the hilt on this occasion. Some time during that steady assault she turned again to look into the mirror. He did too.

'More,' she whispered, her stare fixed on their reflection.

A couple of firm thrusts and she was there, shrieking as the spasms gripped her, almost bouncing her off the banquette. The mirror was great for some things, but when it came to this only staring into Romy's eyes did it for him. But even that wasn't enough for them. It wasn't nearly enough, he concluded as Romy clung to him, her inner muscles clenching violently around him. Picking her up, he maintained a steady rhythm as he pressed her back against the wall.

'More,' he agreed, thrusting into her to a steady beat.

'Again,' she demanded, falling almost immediately.

'You're very greedy,' he observed with satisfaction, taking care to sustain her enjoyment for as long as she could take it.

'Your turn now,' she managed fiercely.

'If you insist,' he murmured, determined to bring her with him.

Romy was a challenge no man could resist and he had not the slightest intention of trying. She was hypersensitive and ultra-needy. She was a willing mate and when he was badly in need of someone who could halfway keep up. Romy could more than keep up.

This was special. This was amazing. Kruz was so considerate, so caring. And she had thought the worst of him. She had badly misjudged him, Romy decided as Kruz steadied her on her feet when they had taken their fill of each other. For now.

'Okay?' he murmured.

Pulling her dress down, she nodded. Feeling increasingly self-conscious, she rescued her briefs and pulled them on.

'I'll take you upstairs to freshen up,' Kruz reassured her as she glanced at her hair in the mirror and grimaced.

Kruz was misunderstood, she decided, leaning on him. Yes, he was hard, but only because he'd had to be. But he could be caring too—under the right circumstances.

'Thanks,' she said, feeling the blush of approval spreading to her ears. 'I'd appreciate a bit of tidy-up before I return to the ballroom.'

She had a reputation for being a hard nut too, but not with Kruz...never with Kruz, she mused, staring up at him through the soft filter of afterglow. Maybe after all this time her heart was alive again. Maybe she was actually learning to trust someone...

They exited the elevator and she quickly realised that the Acostas had taken over the whole floor. There were security guards standing ready to open doors for them, but what she presumed must be Kruz's suite turned out to be an office.

'The bathroom's over there,' he said briskly, pointing in the direction as his attention was claimed by a pretty blond woman who was keen to show him something on her screen.

This wasn't embarrassing, Romy thought as people shot covert glances as her as she made her way between the line of desks.

And if she would insist on playing with fire...
Locking herself in the bathroom, she took a deep,

steadying breath. When would she ever learn that this was nothing more than sex for Kruz, and that she was nothing more than a feeding station for him? And it was too late to worry about what anyone thought.

Running the shower, she stripped off. Stepping under the steaming water felt like soothing balm. She would wash every trace of Kruz Acosta away and harden her resolve towards him as she did so. But nothing helped to ease the ache inside her. It wasn't sexual frustration eating away at her now. It was something far worse. It was as if a seed had been planted the first time they met, and that seed had not only survived but had grown into love.

Love?

Love. What else would you call this certain feeling? And no wonder she had fallen so hard, Romy reasoned, cutting herself some slack as she stepped out of the shower. Kruz was a force of nature. She'd never met anyone like him before.

She was a grown woman who should have known better than to fall for the charms of a man like Kruz—a man who was in no way going to fall at her feet just because she willed it so.

And maybe this grown woman should have checked that there was a towel in the bathroom before she took a shower?

Romy stared around the smart bathroom in disbelief. There was a hand-dryer and that was it. Of course... The hotel had let this as an office, not a bedroom with *en-suite* bathroom. Wasn't that great? How much better could things get?

'Are you ready to go yet?' Kruz bellowed as he hammered on the door.

Fantastic. So now she was the centre of attention of everyone in the office as they waited for her to come out of the bathroom.

'Almost,' she called out brightly, in her most businesslike voice.

Almost? She was standing naked, shivering and dripping all over the floor.

'Couple of minutes,' she added optimistically.

Angling her body beneath a grudging stream of barely warm air wasn't going so well. But there was a grunt from the other side of the door, and retreating footsteps, which she took for a reprieve. Giving up, she called it a day. Slipping on her dress, she ran tense fingers through her mercifully short hair and realised that would have to do. Now all that was left was the walk of shame. Drawing a deep breath, she tilted her chin and opened the door.

Everyone in the office made a point of looking away. *Oh...* She swayed as a wave of faintness washed over her. This was ridiculous. She had never fainted in her life.

'Are you all right, Romy?' Kruz was at her side in an instant with a supporting arm around her shoulders. 'Sit here,' he said, guiding her to a chair when all she longed for was to leave the curious glances far behind. 'I'll get you a glass of water.'

It was a relief when the buzz in the office started up again. She tried to reason away her moment of frailty. She'd hardly drunk anything at the dinner. Had she eaten something earlier that had disagreed with her?

'I'm fine, honestly,' she insisted as Kruz handed her a plastic cup.

'You're clearly not fine,' he argued firmly, 'and I'm going to call you a cab to take you home.'

'But—'

'In fact, I'm going to take you home,' he amended. 'I can't risk you fainting on the doorstep.'

He was going to take her to the tiny terrace she shared with three other girls in a rundown part of town?

Things really couldn't get any better, could they?

She didn't want Kruz to see where she lived. Her aim was one day to live in a tranquil, picturesque area of London by the canal, but for now it was enough to have a roof over her head. She didn't want to start explaining all this to Kruz, or to reveal where her money went. Her mother's privacy was sacrosanct.

She expected Kruz to frown when he saw where she lived. He had just turned his big off-roader into the 'no-go zone', as some of the cabbies called the area surrounding Romy's lodgings. She sometimes had to let them drop her off a couple of streets away, where it was safer for them, and she'd walk the rest of the way home. She wasn't worried about it. She could look after herself. This might look bad to Kruz, but it was home for her as it was for a lot of people.

'What are you doing living here, Romy?'

Here we go. 'Something wrong with it?' she challenged.

Kruz didn't answer. He didn't need to. His face said it all—which was too bad for him. She didn't have to explain herself. She didn't want Kruz Acosta—or anyone else, for that matter—feeling sorry for her. This was something she had chosen to do—*had* to do—took pride in doing. If she couldn't look after her family, what was left?

Stopping the car, Kruz prepared to get out.

'No,' she said. 'I'm fine from here. We're right outside the front door.'

'I'm seeing you in,' he said, and before she could argue with this he was out of the car and slamming the door behind him. Opening her door, he stood waiting. 'This isn't up for discussion,' he growled when she hesitated.

Was anything where Kruz was concerned?

CHAPTER EIGHT

ROMY HAD GOT to him when no one else could.

So why Romy Winner?

Good question, Kruz reflected as he turned the wheel to leave the street where Romy lived. As he joined the wide, brilliantly lit road that led back to the glitter of Park Lane, one of London's classiest addresses, he thought about his office back at the hotel and wondered why he hadn't asked one of his staff to drive her home.

Because Romy was his responsibility. Why make any more of it?

Because seeing her safely through her front door had been vital for him.

Finding out where she lived had been quite a shock. He might have expected her to live in a bohemian area, or even an area on the up, but in the backstreets of a nowhere riddled with crime…?

He was more worried than ever about her now. In spite of Romy's protestations she had still looked pale and faint to him. The kick-ass girl had seemed vulnerable suddenly. The pint-sized warrior wasn't as tough as she thought she was. Which made him feel like a klutz for seducing her in the elevator—even if, to be fair, he had been as much seduced as seducer.

Forgetting sex—*if he could for a moment*—why did Romy live on the wrong side of the tracks when she must make plenty of money? She was one of the most successful photojournalists of her generation. So what was she doing with all the money she earned?

And now, in spite of all his good intentions, as he drew the off-roader to a halt outside the hotel's grandiose pillared entrance, all he could think about was Romy, and how she had left him hungry for more.

She was a free spirit, like him, so why not?

Handing over his keys to the hotel valet, he reasoned that neither of them was interested in emotional ties, but seeing Romy on a more regular basis, as Grace had suggested, would certainly add a little spice to his time in London. His senses went on the rampage at this thought. If Romy hadn't been under par this evening he wouldn't be coming back here on his own now.

She was sick on Monday morning. Violently, sickeningly sick. Crawling back into bed, she pulled the covers over her head and closed her eyes, willing the nausea to go away. She had cleaned her teeth and swilled with mouthwash, but she could still taste bile in her throat.

Thank goodness her housemates had both had early starts that morning, Romy reflected, crawling out of bed some time later. She couldn't make it into work. Not yet, at least. Curling up on the battered sofa in front of the radiator, still in her dressing gown, she groaned as she nursed a cup of mint tea, which was all she could stomach after the latest in a series of hectic trips to the bathroom.

She couldn't be... She absolutely couldn't be—

She wouldn't even think the word. She refused to voice it. She could not be pregnant. Kruz had always used protection.

She had obviously eaten something that disagreed with her. She must have. She had that same lightheaded, bilious feeling that came after eating dodgy food.

Dodgy food at one of London's leading hotels? How likely was that? The Greasy Spoon was famously beyond reproach, and she was Mrs Disinfectant in the kitchen...

Well, *something* had made her feel this way, Romy argued stubbornly as she crunched without enthusiasm on a piece of dry toast.

A glance at the clock reminded her that she didn't have time to sit around feeling sorry for herself; she had a photoshoot with the young star of a reality show this morning, and the greedy maw of *ROCK!*

magazine's picture section, infamously steered by Ronald the Remorseless, wouldn't wait.

Neither would the latest invoice for her mother's nursing care, Romy reflected with concern as she left the house. She had already planned her day around a visit to the nursing home, where she checked regularly on all those things her mother was no longer able to sort out for herself. She had no time to fret. She just had to get on and stop worrying about the improbability of two people who had undergone the same emotional bypass coming together to form a new life.

But...

Okay, so there was a chemist just shy of the *ROCK!* office block.

Dragging in the scent of clean and bright air, Romy assured herself that her visit to the chemist was essential to life, as she needed to stock up on cold and flu remedies. There was quite a lot of that about at the moment. Grabbing a basket, she absent-mindedly popped in a pack of handwipes, a box of tissues, some hairgrips—which she never used—and a torch.

Well, you never know.

Making her way to the counter, she hovered in front of the *'Do you Think you Could be Pregnant?'* section, hoping someone else might push in front of her. Finally palming a pregnancy test, with a look on her face which she hoped suggested that she was very kindly doing it for a friend, she glanced around to make sure there was no one she knew in the shop before approaching the counter. As she reached for her purse the pharmacist came over to help.

'Do you have a quick-fire cure for a stomach upset?' Romy enquired brightly, pushing her purchases towards the woman, with the telltale blue and white box well hidden beneath the other packages.

'Nausea?' the pharmacist asked pleasantly. 'You're not pregnant, are you?' she added, filleting the pile to extract the box containing the pregnancy test with all the sleight of hand of a Pick-up-Sticks champion.

'Of course not.' Romy laughed a little too loudly.

'Are you sure?' The woman's gaze was kind and steady, but her glance did keep slipping to the blue and white packet, which had somehow slithered its way to centre stage. 'I have to know before I can give you any medication…'

'Oh, that's just for a friend,' Romy said, feeling her cheeks blaze.

Meanwhile the queue behind her was growing, and several people were coughing loudly, or tutting.

'I think we'd better err on the side of caution,' the helpful young pharmacist said, reaching behind her to pick up some more packages. 'There are several brands of pregnancy test—'

'I'll take all of them,' Romy blurted.

'And will you come back for the nausea remedy?'

the woman called after her. 'There are some that pregnant women can take—'

Then let those pregnant women take them, Romy thought, gasping with relief as she shut the door of the shop behind her. How ridiculous was this? She didn't even have the courage to buy what she wanted from a chemist now.

'Someone's waiting for you in your office,' the receptionist told her as she walked back into the building.

Not Kruz. Not now. 'Who?' she said warily.

'Kruz Acosta,' the girl said brightly. 'He was here a couple of days ago, wasn't he? Aren't you the lucky one?'

'I certainly am,' Romy agreed darkly. Girding her loins, she headed for the basement.

'Weren't you with him the other night?' someone else chipped in when she stepped into the crowded elevator. 'Great shot of you on the front page of the *West End Chronicle,* Romy,' someone else chirruped. 'In fact, both you and Kruz look amazing…'

General giggling greeted this.

'Can I see?' She leaned over the shoulder of the first girl to look at the newspaper she was holding. *OMG!*

'Oh, that was just a charity thing I attended,' she explained off-handedly, feeling sicker than ever now she'd seen the shot of her and Kruz, slipping not as discreetly as they had thought into the elevator.

Kruz's hand on her back and the expression on her face as she stared up at him both told a very eloquent story. And now there was the type of tension in the lift that suggested the slightest comment from anyone and all the girls would burst out laughing. The banner headline hardly helped: *'Are You Ready for Your Close-Up, Ms Winner?'*

Was that libellous? Romy wondered.

Better not to make a fuss, she concluded, reading on.

'Who doesn't envy Romy Winner her close encounter with elusive billionaire bad-boy Kruz Acosta? Kruz, the only unmarried brother of the four notorious polo-playing Acostas brothers—'

Groaning, she leaned her head against the back of the lift. She didn't need to read any more to know this was almost certainly the reason Kruz was here to see her now. He must hold her wholly responsible for the press coverage. He probably thought she'd set it up. But it took two to tango, Romy reminded herself as she got out of the elevator and strode purposefully towards her cubbyhole.

Breath left her lungs in a rush when she opened the door. Would she *ever* get used to the sight of this man? 'Kruz, I'm—'

'Fantastic!' he exclaimed vigorously. 'How are you this morning, Señorita Winner? Better, I hope?'

'Er…' *Maybe pregnant…maybe not.* 'Good. Thank you,' she said firmly, as if she had to convince herself.

Slipping off her coat, she hung it on the back of the office door. Careful not to touch Kruz, she sidled round the desk. Dumping her bag on the floor at her side, she sat in her swivel chair, relieved to have a tangible barrier between them. Kruz was in jeans, a heavy jacket with the collar pulled up and workmanlike boots—a truly pleasing sight. Especially first thing in the morning…

And last thing at night.

And every other time of day.

Waving to the only other chair in the room—a hard-backed rickety number—she invited him to sit down too. And almost passed out when he was forced to swoop down and move her bag. It was one of those tote things that didn't fasten at the top, and all her purchases were bulging out—including a certain blue and white packet.

'I didn't want to knock your bag over,' he explained, frowning when he saw her expression. 'Still not feeling great?'

Clearly blue and white packets held no significance for a man. 'No…I'm fine,' she said.

'Good,' Kruz said, seeming unconvinced. 'I'm very pleased to hear it.'

So why were his lips still pressed in a frown?
And why was she staring at his mouth?

Suddenly super-conscious of her own lips, and
how it felt to be kissed by Kruz, she dragged her
gaze away. And then remembered the scratch of
his stubble on her skin. The marks probably still
showed—and she had been too distracted by hormonal stuff this morning to remember to cover
them. So everyone had seen them. Double great.

'What can I do for you?' she said.

'You haven't read the article yet?' Kruz queried
with surprise.

He made it impossible for her to ignore the scandal sheet as he laid it out on her desk. 'I like the way
you went after publicity,' he said.

Was that a glint in his wicked black eyes? She put
on a serious act. 'Good,' she said smoothly. 'That's
good...'

'The article starts with the usual nonsense about
you and me,' he reported, leaning over her desk to
point to the relevant passage, 'but then it goes on to
devote valuable column inches to the charity.' He
looked up, his amused dark eyes plumbing deep.
'I'd like to compliment you on having a colleague
standing by.'

'You think I *staged* this?' she exclaimed, morti-
fied that Kruz should imagine she would go to such
lengths.

'Well, didn't you?' he said.

There was a touch of hardness in his expression now, and she was acutely conscious of the pregnancy test peeping out of her bag, mocking her desire to finish this embarrassing interview and find out whether she was pregnant or not. There was also a chance that if Kruz caught sight of the test he might think she had set *him* up too. Sick of all the deception, she decided to come clean.

'I'm not sure how that photograph happened,' she admitted, 'other than to say there are always photojournalists on the look-out for a story—especially at big hotels when there's an important event on. I'm afraid I can't claim any credit for it…' She held Kruz's long, considering stare.

'Well, however it happened,' he said, 'it's done the charity no harm at all. So, well done. Hits on our website have rocketed and donations are flooding in.'

'That *is* great news,' she agreed.

'And funny?' he said.

Perhaps it was hormones making want to giggle. She'd heard it said that Romy Winner would stop at nothing to get a story. She had certainly put her back into it this time.

'So you're not offended by the headline?' she said, reverting to business again.

'It amused me,' Kruz confessed.

Well, that wasn't quite what she'd been hoping for. 'Me too,' she said, as if fun in a lift were all part of the job. 'It's all part of the job,' she said out loud, as if to convince herself it were true.

'Great job,' Kruz murmured, cocking his head with the hint of a smile on his mouth.

'Yes,' she said.

'On the strength of the publicity you've generated so far, I'm going to take you to lunch to discuss further strategy.'

Ah. 'Further strategy?' She frowned. 'Lunch at nine-thirty in the morning?'

She was going to visit her mother later. It was the highlight of her day and one she wouldn't miss for the world. It was also something she couldn't share with Kruz.

'We'll meet at one,' he said, turning for the door.

'No. I can't—'

'You have to eat and so do I,' he said.

'I've got a photoshoot,' she remembered with relief. 'And then—' And then she had finished for the day.

'And then you eat,' Kruz said firmly.

'And then I've got personal business.'

'We'll make it supper, then,' he conceded.

By which time she would know. Vivid images of losing control in the elevator flashed into her head—a telling reminder that she had enjoyed sex with Kruz not once, but many times. And it only took one time for a condom to fail.

They exchanged a few more thoughts and com-

ments about the way forward for the charity, and
then Kruz left her to plunge into a day where nothing went smoothly other than Romy's visit to her
mother. That was like soothing balm after dealing
with a spoiled brat who had screamed for ten types
of soda and sweets with all the green ones taken
out before she would even consider posing for the
camera.

What a day of contrasts it had been, she reflected
later. When she held her mother's soft, limp hand
everything fell into place, and she gained a sense
of perspective, but then it was all quickly lost when
she thought about Kruz and the possibility of being
pregnant.

He studied the report on Romy with interest. She
was certainly good at keeping secrets. But then so
was he. At least this explained why Romy lived
where she did, and why she worked all hours—often
forgetting to eat, according to his sources. Romy
was an only child whose father had died in jail after
the man had left her mother a living corpse after his
final violent attack. Romy was her mother's sole
provider, and had been lucky to come out of that
house alive.

No wonder she was a loner. The violence she had
witnessed as a child should have put her off men for
life, but it certainly went some way to explaining
why Romy snatched at physical relief whilst shun-

ning anything deeper. There had been brief relationships, but nothing significant. He guessed her ability
to trust hovered around zero. Which made *him* the
last partner on earth for her—not that he was thinking of making his relationship with Romy anything
more than it already was. His capacity for offering
a woman more than physical relief was also zero.

They made a good pair, he reflected, flinging the
document aside, but it wasn't a good pairing in the
way Romy wanted it to be. He'd seen how she looked
at him, and for the first time in his life he wished
he had something to offer. But he had learned long
ago it was only possible to survive, to achieve and
to develop, to do any of those things, if emotion
was put aside. It was far better, in his opinion, to
feel nothing and move forward than look back, remember and break.

CHAPTER NINE

WHAT A CRAZY day. Up. Down. And all points in between. And it wasn't over yet. The blue and white packet was still sitting where she had left it on the bathroom shelf, and after that she had supper with Kruz to look forward to—and no way of knowing how it would go.

But her meeting with Kruz would be on neutral territory, Romy reminded herself as she soaped down in the tiny shower stall back at the house she shared with the other girls. She would be in public with him. What was the worst that could happen?

The reporter from the scandal sheet might track them down again?

Kruz had seemed to find that amusing. So why hadn't she?

The thought that Kruz meant so much to her and she didn't mean a thing to him hurt. She'd never been in this position before. She'd always been able to control her feelings. She certainly didn't waste them. She cared for her mother, and for her friends, but where men were concerned—there were no men. And now of all the men in the world she'd had to fall for Kruz Acosta, who had never pretended to be anything more than an entertaining companion with special skills—a man who treated sex like food. He needed it. He enjoyed it. But that didn't mean he remembered it beyond the last meal.

While *she* remembered every detail of what he'd said and how he'd said it, how he'd looked at her, how he'd touched her, and how he'd made her feel. It wasn't just sex for the sake of a quick fix for her. It was meaningful. And it had left her defences in tatters.

More fool her.

She was not going slinky tonight, Romy decided in the bedroom. She was going to wear her off-duty uniform of blue jeans, warm sweater and a floppy scarf draped around her neck.

Glancing at her reflection in the mirror, she was satisfied there was nothing provocative about her appearance that Kruz could possibly misinterpret. She looked as if she was going for supper with a friend, which in some ways she was, but first she had something to do—and the sooner she got it over and done with the sooner she would know.

She already knew.

He stood up and felt a thrill as Romy walked into the steak bar. She looked amazing. She always did to him.

'Romy,' he said curtly, hiding those thoughts. 'Good to see you. Please sit down. We've got a lot I'd like to get through tonight, as I'm going to be away for a while. Before I go I need to be sure we're both singing from the same hymn sheet. Red wine or white?'

She looked at him blankly.

'It's a simple question. Red or white?'

'Er—orange juice, please.'

'Whatever you like.' He let it go. Whatever was eating Romy, it couldn't be allowed to get in the way of their discussion tonight. There was a lot he wanted to set straight—like the budgets that she had to work to.

The waiter handed Romy a menu and she began to study it, while he studied her. After reading the report on Romy he understood a lot more about her. He saw the gentleness she hid so well behind the steel, and the capacity for caring above and beyond anything he could ever have imagined. He jerked his gaze away abruptly. He needed this upcoming trip. He needed space from this woman. No one distracted him like Romy, and he had a busy life—polo, the Acosta family interests, *his* business interests. He had no time to spare for a woman.

To make the break he had arranged a tour of his offices worldwide, with a grudge match with Nero Caracas at the end of it to ease any remaining frustration. A battle between his own Band of Brothers polo team and Nero's Assassins would be more than enough to put his life back in focus, he concluded as Romy laid down the menu and stared at him.

'You're going away?' she said.

'Yes,' he confirmed briskly. 'So, if you're ready to order, let's get back to the agenda. We've got a lot to get through tonight.'

The food was good. He ate well.

Romy picked at her meal and seemed preoccupied.

'Do I?' she said when he asked her about it.

She gave a thin smile to the waiter as she accepted a dessert menu. She'd hardly eaten anything.

'Coffee and ice cream?' he suggested when the waiter returned to take their order. 'They make the best of both here. The ice cream's home-made on the premises—fresh cream and raw eggs.'

She blinked. 'Neither, thank you. I think I've got everything I need here,' she said, collecting up her things as if she couldn't wait to go.

'I'll call for the bill.' This was not the ending to the night he had envisaged. Yes, he needed space from Romy—but on his own terms, and to a time-table that suited him.

Business and pleasure don't mix, he reflected wryly as she left the table, heading for the door. When would he ever learn? But, however many miles he put between them, something told him he would never be far enough away from Romy to put her out of his head.

* * *

She guessed shock had made her sick this time. It must be shock. It was only ten o'clock in the evening and she had just brought up every scrap of her picked-over meal. Shock at Kruz going away—just like that, without a word of warning. No explanation at all.

And why would he tell her?

She was nothing to him, Romy realised, shivering as she pulled the patchwork throw off her bed to wrap around her shaking shoulders. She was simply a photographer the Acostas had tasked with providing images for their charitable activities—a photographer who had lost her moral compass on a grassy bank, a press coach and in an elevator. *Classy.* So why hadn't she spoken out tonight? Why hadn't she said something to Kruz? There had been more than one opportunity for her to be straight with him.

About this most important of topics she had to be brutally honest with herself first. This wasn't a business matter she could lightly discuss with Kruz, or even a concern she had about working for the charity. This was a child—a life. This was a new life depending on her to make the right call.

Swivelling her laptop round, she studied the shots she'd taken of Kruz. Not one of them showed a flicker of tenderness or humour. He was a hard, driven man. How would he take the news? She couldn't just blurt out, *You're going to be a daddy,* and expect him to cheer. She wouldn't do that, anyway. The fact that she was having Kruz's baby was so big, so life-changing for both of them, so precious and tender to her, she would choose her moment. She only wished things could be different between them—but wishing didn't make things happen. Actions made things happen, and right now she needed to make money more than she ever had.

As she flicked through the saleable images she hadn't yet offered on the open market, she realised there were plenty—which was a relief. And there were also several elevator shots on the net to hold interest. Thank goodness no one had been around for the grassy bank…

She studied the close-ups of her and Kruz as they had been about to get into the elevator and smiled wryly. They made a cool couple.

And now the cool couple were going to have a baby.

He ground his jaw with impatience as his sister-in-law gave him a hard time. He'd stopped over at the *estancia* in Argentina and appreciated the space. He was no closer to sorting out his feelings for Romy and would have liked more time to do so. The irony of having so many forceful women in one family had not escaped him. Glancing at his wristwatch, he toyed with the idea of inventing a meeting so he had an excuse to end the call.

'Are you still there, Kruz?'

'I'm still here, Grace,' he confirmed. 'But I have pressing engagements.'

'Well, make sure you fit Romy into them,' Grace insisted, in no way deterred.

'I might have to go away again. Can't you liaise with her?'

'And choose which photographs we want to use?'

He swore beneath his breath. 'Forgive me, Grace, but you're in London and I'm not right now.'

'I'll liaise with Romy on one condition,' his wily sister-in-law agreed.

'And that is?' he demanded.

'You see her again and sort things out between you.'

'Can't do that, Grace. Thousands of miles between us,' he pointed out.

'So send for her,' Grace said, as if this were normal practise rather than dramatic in the extreme. 'I've heard the way your voice changes when you talk about Romy. What are you afraid of, Kruz?'

'Me? Afraid?' he scoffed.

'Even men like Nacho have hang-ups—before he met me, that is,' his sister-in-law amended with warmth and humour in her voice. 'Don't let your hang-ups spoil things for you, Kruz. At least speak to her. Promise me?'

He hummed and hawed, and then agreed. What

was all the rush about? Romy could just as easily have got in touch with *him*.

Maybe there were reasons?

What reasons?

Maybe her mother was ill. If that were the case he would be concerned for her. Romy's care of her mother was exemplary, according to his investigations. He hadn't thought to ask about her. Grace was right. The least he could do was call Romy and find out.

'Kruz?'

She had to stop hugging the phone as if it were a lifeline. She had to stop analysing every microsecond of his all too impersonal greeting. She had to accept the fact that Kruz was calling her because he wanted to meet for an update on the progress she was making with the banners, posters and flyers for the upcoming charity polo match. She had to get real so she could do the job she was being paid to do. This might all be extra to her work for *ROCK!*, but she had no intention of short-changing either the magazine or the Acosta family. She believed in the Acosta charity and she was going to give it everything she'd got.

'Of course we can meet—no, there's no reason why not.' Except her heart was acting up. It was one thing being on the other end of a phone to Kruz, but being in the same room as him, which was what he seemed to be suggesting…

'Can you pack and come tomorrow?'

'Come where?'

'To the *estancia*, of course.'

Shock coursed through her. 'You're calling me from Argentina? When you said you were going away I had no idea you were going to Argentina.'

'Does that make a difference?' Kruz demanded. 'I'll send the jet—what's your problem, Romy?'

You. 'Kruz, I work—'

'You gave me to understand you were almost self-employed now and could please yourself.'

'Sort of…'

'Sort of?' he queried. 'Are you or aren't you? If your boss at *ROCK!* acts up, check to see if you've got some holiday owing. Just take time off and get out here.'

So speaks the wealthy man, Romy thought, flicking quickly through the diary in her mind.

'Romy?' Kruz prompted impatiently. 'Is there a reason why you can't come here tomorrow?'

Pregnant women were allowed to travel, weren't they? 'No,' she said bluntly. 'There's no reason why I can't travel.'

'See you tomorrow.'

She stared at the dead receiver in her hand. To be in Argentina tomorrow might sound perfectly normal to a jet-setting polo player, but even to a newshound like Romy it sounded reckless. And it gave her no chance to prepare her story, she realised, staring at an e-mail from Kruz containing her travel details that had already flashed up on her screen. Not that she needed a story, Romy reassured herself as she scanned the arrangements he had made for her to board his private jet. She would just tell him the truth. Yes, they had used protection, but a condom must have failed.

Sitting back, she tried to regret what had happened—was happening—and couldn't. How could she regret the tiny life inside her? Mapping her stomach with her hands, she realised that all she regretted was wasting her feelings on Kruz—a man who walked in and out of her life at will, leaving her as isolated as she had ever been.

Like countless other women who had to make do and mend with what life had dealt them.

She would just have to make do and mend *this,* Romy concluded.

Having lost patience with her maudlin meanderings, she tapped out a brief and businesslike reply to Kruz's e-mail. She didn't have to sleep with him. She could resist him. It was just a matter of being sensible. The main thing was to do a good job for the charity and leave Argentina with her pride intact. She would find the right moment to tell Kruz about the baby. They were two civilised human beings and would work it out. She would be on that flight tomorrow, she would finish the job Grace had given her, and then she would decide the way ahead as she always had. Just as she had protected her mother for as long as she could, she would now protect her unborn child. And if that meant facing up to Kruz and telling him how things were going to be from here on in, then that was exactly what she was going to do.

The flight was uneventful. In fact it was soothing compared to what awaited her, Romy suspected, resting back. She tried to soothe herself further by reflecting on all the good things that had happened. She had worked hard to establish herself as a free-lance alongside her magazine work, and her photographs had featured in some of the glossies as the product of someone who was more than just a member of the paparazzi. One of her staunchest supporters had turned out to be Ronald, who had made her cry—baby-head, she realised—when he'd said that he believed in her talent and expected her to go far.

Well, she was going far now, Romy reflected, blowing out a long, thoughtful breath as she considered the journey ahead of her. And as to what lay on the other side of that flight… She could only guess that this pampering on a private jet, with freshly squeezed orange juice on tap, designer food and cream kidskin seats large enough to curl up and snooze on, would be the calm before the storm.

Tracing the curve of her stomach protectively as the jet circled before swooping down to land on the Acostas' private landing strip, Romy felt her heart bump when she spotted the *hacienda*, surrounded by endless miles of green with the mountains beyond. The scenery in this part of Argentina was ravishingly beautiful, and the *hacienda* nestled in its grassy frame in such a favoured spot. Bathed in sunlight, the old stone had turned a glinting shade of molten bronze. The pampas was only a wilderness to those who couldn't see the beauty in miles of fertile grass, or to those with no appreciation of the varied wildlife and birdlife that called this place home.

She craned her neck to catch a glimpse of thundering waterfalls crashing down from the Andes and lazy rivers moving like glittering ribbons towards the sea. It made her smile to see how many horses were grazing on the pampas, and her heart thrilled at the sight of the *gauchos* working amongst the herds of Criolla ponies. They were no more than tiny dots as the jet came in to land, and the ponies soon scattered when they heard the engines. She wondered if Kruz was among the riders chasing them...

She was pleased to be back.

The realisation surprised her. She must be mad, knowing what lay ahead of her, Romy concluded as the seatbelt sign flashed on, but against all that was logical this felt like coming home.

After flying overnight, she stepped out of the

plane into dry heat on a beautifully sunny day. The sky was bright blue and decorated with clouds that looked like cotton wool balls. The scent of grass and blossom was strong, though it was spoiled a little by the tang of aviation fuel. Slipping on her sunglasses, Romy determined that nothing was going to spoil her enjoyment of this visit. This was a fabulous country, with fabulous people, and she couldn't wait to start taking pictures.

There was a *gaucho* standing next to a powerful-looking truck, which he had parked on the grass verge to one side of the airstrip, but there was no sign of Kruz. She should be relieved about that. It would give her time to settle in, Romy reasoned as the weather-beaten *gaucho* came to greet her. He introduced himself as Alessandro, explaining that Kruz was away from the *estancia*.

Would Kruz be away for a long time? Romy wondered, not liking to ask. Anyway, it was good to know that he wasn't crowding her. *But she missed him.*

Hard luck, she thought wryly as the elderly ranch-hand pointed away across the vast sea of grass. Ah, so Kruz wasn't *staying* away—he was out riding on the pampas. Her heart lifted, but then she reasoned that he must have seen the jet coming into land, yet wouldn't put himself out to come and meet her.

That was good, she told herself firmly. No pressure.

No caring, either.

She stood back as Alessandro took charge of her luggage. 'You mustn't lift anything in your condition,' he said.

She blushed furiously. Was her pregnancy so obvious? She was wearing jeans with a broad elastic panel at the front, and over the top of them a baggy T-shirt *and* a fashionable waterfall cardigan, which the salesgirl had assured Romy was guaranteed to hide her small bump. *Wrong,* Romy concluded. If Alessandro could tell she was pregnant, there would be no hiding the fact from Kruz.

Perhaps people were just super tuned-in to nature out here on the pampas, she reflected as Alessandro opened the door of the cab for her and stood back. Climbing in, she sat down. Breathing a sigh of relief as the elderly *gaucho* closed the door, she took a moment to compose herself. The interlude was short-lived. As she turned to smile at Alessandro when he climbed into the driver's seat at her side her heart lurched at the sight of Kruz, riding flat out across the pampas towards them.

It struck her as odd that she had never seen such a renowned horseman riding before, but then they actually knew very little about what made each other tick. At this distance Kruz was little more than a dark shadow, moving like an arrow towards her, but it was as if her heart had told her eyes to look for him and here he was. Her spirits rose as she watched him draw closer. Surely a man who was so at one with nature would be thrilled at the prospect of bringing new life into the world?

So why did she feel so apprehensive?

She should be apprehensive, Romy concluded, nursing her bump. This baby meant everything to her, and she would fight for the right to keep her child with her whatever a powerful man like Kruz Acosta had to say about it, but she couldn't imagine he would make things easy for her.

'And now we wait,' Alessandro said, settling back as he turned off the engine.

He had promised himself he would stay out of Romy's way until the evening, giving her a chance to settle in. He wanted her know she wasn't at the top of his list of priorities for the day. Which clearly explained why he was riding across the pampas now, with his sexual radar on red alert. No one excited him like Romy. No one intrigued him as she did. Life was boring without her, he had discovered. Other women were pallid and far too eager to please him. He had missed Romy's fiery temperament—amongst other things—and the way she never shirked from taking him on.

Reining in, he allowed his stallion to approach the truck at a high-stepping trot. Halting, he dismounted. His senses were already inflamed at the sight of her, sitting in the truck. The moment the jet had appeared in the sky, circling overhead, he had turned for home, knowing an end to his physical ache was at last in sight.

Striding over to the truck, he forgot all his good intentions about remaining cool and threw open the passenger door. 'Romy—'

'Kruz,' she said, seeming to shrink back in her seat.

This was not the reception he had anticipated. And why was she hugging herself like that? 'I'll see you at the house,' he said, speaking to Alessandro. Slamming the passenger door, he slapped the side of the truck and went back to his horse.

He could wait, he told himself as he cantered back to the *hacienda*. The house was empty. He had given the housekeepers the day off. He wanted the space to do with as he liked—to do with Romy as he liked.

He stabled the horse before returning to the house. He found Romy in the kitchen, where Alessandro was pouring her a cold drink. The old man was fussing over her like a mother hen. He had never seen that before.

'Romy is perfectly capable of looking after herself,' he said, tugging off his bandana to wipe the dust of riding from his face.

As Alessandro grunted he took another look at Romy, who was seated at the kitchen table, side on to him. She seemed small—smaller than he remembered—but her jaw was set as if for battle. So be it.

After his shower he would be more than happy to accommodate her.

'Journey uncomfortable?' he guessed, knowing how restless *he* became if he was caged in for too enough.

'Not at all,' she said coolly, still without turning to face him.

'I'm going to take a shower,' he said, thinking her rude, 'and then I'll brief you on the photographs Grace wants you to take.'

'Romy needs to rest first.'

He stared at Alessandro. The old man had never spoken to him like that before—had never danced attendance on a woman in all the years he'd known him.

'I'd love a shower too,' Romy said, springing up.

'Fine. See you later at supper,' he snapped, mouthing, *What?* as Alessandro gave him a sharp look. And then, to his amazement, his elderly second-in-command took hold of Romy's bags and led the way out of the kitchen and up the stairs. 'Maria has prepared the front room overlooking the corral,' he yelled after them.

Neither one of them replied.

'What the hell is going on?' he demanded, the moment Alessandro returned.

'You had better ask Señorita Winner that question,' his old *compadre* told him, heading for the door.

'You know—*you* tell me.'

The old *gaucho* answered this with a shrug as he went out through the door.

She shouldn't have left the door to her bedroom open, Romy realised, stirring sleepily. It wasn't wide open, but it was open enough to appear inviting. She had meant to close it, but had fallen asleep on the bed after her shower. Jet-lag and baby-body, she supposed. She needed a siesta these days.

She needed more than that. Holly Acosta had warned her about this phase of pregnancy…hormones running riot…the 'sex-mad phase', Holly had dubbed it, Romy remembered, clutching her pillow as she tried to forget.

Maybe she had left the door open on purpose, Romy concluded as Kruz, still damp from his shower and clad only in a towel, strolled into the room. Maybe she had deluded herself that they could have one last hurrah and then she would tell him. But she had not expected this surge of feeling as her body warmed in greeting. She had not expected Kruz simply to walk into the room expecting sex, or that she would feel quite so ready to oblige him. What had happened to all those bold resolutions about remaining chaste until she had told him about the baby?

She didn't speak. She didn't need to. She just made room for him on the bed. She was well covered in a sheet—which was more than could be said for

Kruz. Her throat felt as if it was tied in knots when the towel he had tucked around his waist dropped to the floor.

Settling down on the bed, he kept some tantalising, teasing space between them, while she covered the evidence of her pregnancy with the bedding. Resting on one elbow, he stared into her eyes, and at that moment she would have done anything for him.

Anything.

He toyed with her hair, teasing her with the delay, while she turned her face to brush her lips along his hand. Remembered pleasure was a strong driver—the strongest. She wanted him. She couldn't hide it. She didn't want to. Her body had more needs now than ever before.

'You've put on weight, Romy,' he murmured, suckling on her breasts. 'Don't,' he complained when she tried to stop him, nervous that Kruz might take his interest lower. 'The added weight suits you. I meant it as a compliment.'

Kruz was in a hurry—which was good. She wasn't even sure he noticed the distinct swell of her belly on his way to his destination. She was all sensation…all want and need…with only one goal in mind. She wasn't even sure whether Kruz pressed her legs apart or whether she opened them for him. She only knew that she was resting back on a soft bank of pillows while he held her thighs apart. And when he bent to his task he was so good… Lacing her fingers through his hair, she decided he was a master of seduction—not that she needed much persuasion. He was so skilled. His tongue... His hands... His understanding of her needs and responses was so acute, so knowing, so—

He paused to protect them both. She thought about telling him then, but it would have been ridiculous, and anyway the hunger was raging inside her now. She wanted him. He wanted her. It was a need so deep, so primal, that nothing could stop them now. She groaned as he sank deep. This was so good—it felt so right. Kruz set up a rhythm, which she followed immediately, mirroring his moves, but with more fire, more need, more urgency.

'That's right—come for me, baby.'

She didn't need any encouragement and fell blindly, violently, triumphantly, with screaming, keening, groaning relief. And Kruz kissed her all the while, his strong arms holding her safe as she tumbled fast and hard. His firm mouth softened to whisper of encouragement as he made sure she enjoyed every second of it before he even thought of taking his own pleasure. When he did it raised her erotic temperature again. Just seeing him enjoying her was enough to do that. The pleasure was never-ending, and as wave after wave after wave of almost unbearable sensation washed over her it was Kruz who kept her safe to abandon herself to this unbelievable union of body and soul.

Sensation and emotion combined had to be the most powerful force any human being could tap into, she thought, still groaning with pleasure as she slowly came down. Clinging to Kruz, nestling against his powerful body, left her experiencing feelings so strong, so beautiful, she could hardly believe they were real. She smiled as she kissed him, moving to his shoulders, to his chest, to his neck. After such brutally enjoyable pleasure this was a rare tender moment to treasure. A life-changing moment, she thought as Kruz continued to tend to her needs.

'Romy?'

She sensed the change in him immediately.

'What?' she murmured. But she already knew, and felt a chill run through her when Kruz lifted his head. The look in his eyes told her everything she needed to know. They were black with fury.

'When were you planning to tell me?' he said.

CHAPTER TEN

SHE HAD EVERY reason to hate the condemnation in Kruz's black stare. She loved her child already. Yes, cool, hard, emotionless Romy Winner had turned into a soft, blobby cocoon overnight. But still with warrior tendencies, she realised as she wriggled up the bed. If he wanted a fight she was ready.

Two of them had made this baby, and their child was a precious life she was prepared to defend with her own life. She surprised herself with how immediately her priorities could change. She wasn't alone any more. It would never be just about her again. She was a mother. In hindsight, she had been mad to think Kruz wouldn't notice she was pregnant. The swell of her belly was small, but growing bigger every day, as if the child they'd made together was as proud and strong as its parents.

She was happy to admit her guilt. She *was* guilty of backing away at the first hurdle and not telling Kruz right away. Allowing him to find out like this way was a terrible thing to do. It had been seeing him and forgetting everything in the moment…

'Are you ashamed of the baby?' he said. Springing into a sitting position, he loomed over her, a terrifying powerhouse of suppressed outrage.

Before her mouth had a chance to form words he detached himself from her arms and swung off the bed. Striding across the room, he closed the door on the bathroom and she heard him run the shower. He was shocked and she was frantic. Her mind refused to cooperate and tell her what to do next. She'd really messed up, and now she would be caught in the whirlwind.

He'd been away, she reasoned as she listened to Kruz in the bathroom.

There was the telephone. There was the internet. There was always a way of getting hold of someone. She just hadn't tried.

They didn't have that kind of relationship.

What *did* they have?

She hadn't been prepared for pregnancy because she'd had no reason to suppose she was in line to make a baby.

You had sex, didn't you?

The brutal truth. They'd had sex vigorously and often. Two casual acquaintances coming together for no other purpose than mindless pleasure until the charity gave them a common aim. They had enjoyed each other greedily and thoughtlessly, with only a mind to that pleasure. Maybe Kruz thought she was going to hit him with a paternity suit. Holly had explained to her once that the Acostas were so close and kept the world at bay because massive wealth brought massive risk. They found it hard to trust anyone, because most people had an agenda.

'Kruz—'

She flinched as the door opened and quickly wrapped the sheet around her. Yet again she was wasting time thinking when she should be doing. She should have got dressed and then she could face him as an equal, rather than having to try and tug the sheet from the bottom of the bed so she could retain what little dignity was left to her.

'No— Wait—' Kruz had pulled on his jeans and top and was heading for the door. Somehow she managed to yank the sheet free and stumble towards him. 'Please—I realise this must be a terrible shock for you, but we really have to talk.'

'A *shock*?' he said icily, staring down at her hand on his arm.

She recoiled from him. Suddenly Kruz's arm felt like the arm of a stranger, while she felt like a hysterical woman accosting someone she didn't know.

She tried again—calmly this time. 'Please… We must talk.'

'*Now* we need to talk?' he said mildly.

She had hurt him. But it was so much more than that. Kruz was shocked—felled by the enormity of what she'd been keeping from him. His brain was scrambled. She could tell he needed space. 'Please...' she said gently, trying to appeal to a softer side of him.

'No,' he rapped, pulling away. 'No,' he said again, shaking her off. 'You can't just hit me with this and expect me to produce a ready-made plan.'

She didn't expect anything from him, but she couldn't just let him turn his back and walk away. Moving in front of him, she leaned against the door. 'Well, that's up to you. I can't stop you leaving.'

Kruz's icy expression assured her this was the case.

'I don't want anything from you,' she said, trying to subdue the tremor in her voice. 'I know a baby isn't a good enough reason for us to stay together in some sort of mismatched hook-up—'

'I wasn't aware we were *planning* to hook up,' he cut in with a quiet intensity that really scared her.

She moved away from the door. What else could she do? She felt dead inside. She should have told him long before now, but Kruz's reaction to finding out had completely thrown her. They were both responsible for a new life, but he seemed determined to shut that fact out. She would have to speak to him through lawyers when she got back to England, and somehow she would have to complete her work for the charity while she was here in Argentina—with or without Kruz Acosta's co-operation.

Needing isolation and time to think, she hurried to the bathroom and shut the door—just in time to hear Kruz close the outer door behind him.

No! No! No! This could not be happening. He micro-managed every aspect of his life to make sure something unexpected could never blindside him. So how? Why now?

Why ever?

With no answers that made sense he stalked in the direction of the stables.

A child? *His* child? His baby?

His mind was filled with wonder. But having a child was unthinkable for him. It was a gift he could never accept. He couldn't share his nightmares—not with Romy and much less with an innocent child. Who knew what he was capable of?

In the army they'd said there were three kinds of soldiers: those who were trained to kill and couldn't bring themselves to do it; those who were trained to kill and enjoyed it; and those who were trained to kill and did so because it was their duty. They did that duty on auto-pilot, without allowing themselves to think. He had always thought that last type of soldier was the most dangerous and the most damned, because they had only one choice. That was to live their lives after the army refusing to remember, refusing to feel, refusing to face what they'd done. He was that soldier.

There was only one option open to him. He would allow Romy to complete her work here and then he would send her back. He would provide for the child and for Romy. He would write a detailed list of everything she must have and then he would hand that list over to his PA.

From the first night he had woken screaming he had vowed never to inflict his nightmares on anyone. The things he'd witnessed—the things he'd done—none of that was remotely acceptable to him in the clear light of peace. He was damned for all time. He had been claimed by the dark side, which was the best reason he knew to keep himself aloof from decent people. He could not allow himself to feel anything for Romy, or for their child—not unless he wanted to damage them both. The best, the *only* thing he could do to protect them was to step out of Romy's life.

The mechanical function of tacking up his stallion soothed him and set his decision in stone. The great beast and he would share the wild danger of a gallop across the pampas. They both needed to break free, to run, to seize life without thought or plan for what might lay ahead.

He rode as far as the river and then kicked his booted feet out of the stirrups. Throwing the reins over the stallion's head, he dismounted. All he could see wherever he looked was Romy, and all he could hear was her voice. The apprehension and concern in her eyes was as clear now as if she were standing in front of him. She was frightened she wasn't ready for a baby. *He* would never be ready. His family, who tolerated him, knew more than most people did about him, was enough.

Tipping his face to the sun, he realised this was the first time he had ever backed away from any challenge. He normally met each one head-on. But this tiny unborn child had stopped him dead in his tracks without a road map or a solution. He didn't question the fact that the child was his. The little he knew about Romy gave him absolute trust in what she told him. Whistling up his stallion, he sprang into the saddle and turned for home.

She packed her case and then left the *hacienda* to take the shots she needed for Grace. She knelt and waited silently on the riverbank for what felt like hours for the flocks of birds feeding close by to wheel and soar like ribbons in the sky. She could only marvel at their beauty. It gave her a sort of peace which she hoped would transmit to the baby.

There was no perfect world, Romy concluded. There were only perfect moments like this, populated by imperfect human beings like herself and Kruz, who were just trying to make the best of their journey through life. It was no use wishing she could share this majestic beauty with their child. She would never be invited to Argentina. She might never see the snow-capped Andes and smell the lush green grass again, but her photographs would remind her of the wild land the father of her child inhabited.

Hoisting her kitbag onto her shoulder, she started back to the *hacienda*. She had barely reached the courtyard when she saw Kruz riding towards her. She loved him. It was that simple. Turning in the opposite direction, she kept her head down and walked rapidly away. She wasn't ready for this.

Would she ever be ready for this?

She stopped and changed direction, following him round to the stables, where she found him dismounting. Without acknowledging her presence, he led the stallion past her.

He had been calm, Kruz realised. The ride had calmed him. But seeing Romy again had shaken him to the core. He wanted her—and more than in just a sexual way. He wanted to put his arm around her and share her worries and excitement, to see where the road took them. But Romy's life wasn't an experiment he could dip into. He might not be able to shake the feeling that they belonged together, but the only safe thing for Romy was to put her out of his life.

'Kruz...'

He lifted the saddle onto the fence and started taking his horse's bridle off.

'How could I go to bed with you, knowing I was pregnant,' she said, 'and yet say nothing?'

Her voice, soft and shaking slightly, touched him somewhere deep. He turned to find her frowning. 'Don't beat yourself up about it,' he said without expression. 'What's done is done.'

'And cannot be undone,' she whispered as the stallion turned a reproachful gaze on him. 'Not that I...'

As her voice faded his gaze slipped to her stomach, where the swell of pregnancy was quite evident on her slender frame. In his rutting madness he had chosen not to see it. He felt guilty now.

The stallion whickered and nuzzled him imperatively, searching for a mint. He found one and the stallion took it delicately from his hand. Clicking his tongue, he tried to move the great beast on, but his horse wasn't going anywhere. As of this moment, one small girl with her chin jutting out had half a ton of horseflesh bending to her will.

'He needs feeding,' he said without emotion as he waited for Romy to move aside.

'I have needs too,' she said, but her soft heart put the horse first, and so she moved, allowing him to lead the stallion to his stable.

'Are you going to make me wait as I made you wait?' she said as she watched him settle the horse.

He was checking its hooves, but lifted his head to look at her.

'Okay, I get it—you're not so petty,' she said. 'But we do have to talk some time, Kruz.'

He returned to what he'd been doing without a word.

She waited by the stable door, watching Kruz looking after his big Criolla. What she wouldn't do for a moment of that studied care…

So what are you standing around for?

'Can I—'

'Can you what?' he said, still keenly aware of her, apparently, even though he had his back turned to her.

'Can I come in and give him a mint?' she asked.

The few seconds' pause felt like an hour.

'Hold your hand out flat,' he said at last.

She took the mint, careful not to touch Kruz more than she had to. Her heart thundered as he stood back. There was nothing between her and the enormous horse that just stood motionless, staring at her unblinking. Her throat felt dry, and her heart was thundering, but then, as if a decision had been made, the stallion's head dropped and its velvet lips tickled her palm. Surprised by its gentleness, she stroked its muzzle. The prickle of whiskers made her smile, and she went on to stroke its sleek, shiny neck. The warmth was soothing, and the contact between them made her relax.

'You're a beauty, aren't you?' she whispered.

Conscious that Kruz was watching her, she stood back and let him take over. He made the horse quiver with pleasure as he groomed it with long, rhythmical strokes. She envied the connection between them.

She waited until Kruz straightened up before saying, 'Can we talk?'

'You're *asking* me?' he said, brushing past her to put the tack away.

His voice was still cold, and she felt as if she had blinked and opened her eyes to find the last few minutes had been a dream and now it was back to harsh reality. But her pregnancy wasn't something she could put to one side. Now it was out in the open she had to see this through, and so she followed Kruz to the tackroom and closed the door behind them. He swung around and, leaning back against the wall, with a face that was set and unfriendly, waited for her to speak.

'I would have told you sooner, if—'

'If you hadn't been climbing all over me?' he suggested in a chilly tone.

She lifted her chin. 'I didn't notice you taking a back seat at the time.'

'So when were you going to tell me that you're pregnant?'

'You seem more concerned about my faults than our child. There were so many times when I wanted to tell you—'

'But your needs were just too great?' he said, regarding her with a face she didn't recognize—a face that was closed off to any possibility of understanding between them.

'I remember my need being as great as yours,'

she said. 'Anyway, I don't want to argue with you about this, Kruz. I want to discuss what has happened while we've got the chance. For God's sake, Kruz—what's wrong with you? Anyone would think you were trying to drive me away—taking *your* child with me.'

'You'll stay here until I tell you to go,' he said, snatching hold of her arm.

'Let me go,' she cried furiously.

'There's nowhere for you to go—there's just thousands of miles of nothing out there .'

'I'm leaving Argentina.'

'And then what?' he demanded.

'And then I'll make a life for me and our baby— the baby you don't care to acknowledge.'

Was that a flicker of something human in his eyes? Had she got through to him at last? His grip had relaxed on her arm.

It was a feint of which any fighter would be proud. Kruz was still hot from his ride, still unshaven and dusty, and when his mouth crashed down on hers she knew she should fight him off, but instead she battled to keep him close.

'It's that easy, isn't it?' he snarled, thrusting her away. '*You're* that easy.'

She confronted him angrily. 'You shouldn't have kissed me. You shouldn't have doubted me.' She paused a beat and shook her head. 'And I should have told you sooner than I did.'

'You kissed me back,' he said, turning for the door.

Yes, she had. And she would kiss him again, Romy realised as heat, hope and longing surged inside her. What did that make her? Deluded?

'Where are you going?' she demanded as Kruz opened the door. 'We have to talk this through.'

'I'm done talking, Romy.'

Moving ahead of him, she pressed herself against the door like a barricade. 'I'm just as scared as you are,' she admitted.

'You? Scared?' he said.

'We didn't plan this, Kruz, but however unready we are to become parents, we're no different than thousands of other couples. Whether we're ready or not, in less than a year our lives will be turned upside down by a baby.'

'*Your* life, maybe,' he snapped.

His eyes were so cold…his face was so closed off to her. 'Kruz—'

'I need time to think,' he said sharply.

'No,' she fired back. 'We need to talk about this now.'

Pressing against the door, she refused to move. She was going to say what she had to say and then she would leave Argentina for good.

'There's nothing for you to think about,' she said firmly. 'The baby and I don't need you—and we certainly don't want your money. When I get back to England I'll speak to my lawyers and make sure you have fair access to our child. But that's it. Don't think for one moment that I can't provide everything a baby needs and more.'

The blood drained from his face. He was furious, but Kruz contained his feelings, which made him seem all the more threatening. Her hands flew to cradle her stomach. She was right to feel apprehensive. She had no lawyers, while Kruz probably had a whole team waiting on him. And she had to find somewhere decent to live. For all her brave talk she was in no way ready to welcome a baby into the world yet.

'Do you mind?' he said coldly, staring behind her at the door.

Standing aside, she let him go. What else could she do? She had no more cards to play. If Kruz didn't want any part in the life of his child then she wasn't going to beg. She couldn't pretend it didn't hurt to think he could just brush her off like this. She understood that he guarded his privacy fiercely, but the birth of a baby was a life-changing event for both of them.

But this was day one of her life as a single mother, so she had to get over it. With the lease about to run out on her rented house, she couldn't afford to be downhearted. Her priority was to find somewhere to live. So what if she couldn't afford the area she loved? She maybe never would be able to afford it.

She could still find somewhere safe and respectable. She would work all hours to make that happen.

She waited in the shadowy warmth of the tackroom, breathing in the pleasant aroma of saddle soap and horse until she was sure Kruz was long gone, and then she walked out into the brilliant sunlight of the yard to find the big stallion still watching her, with his head resting over the stable door.

'I've made a mess of everything, haven't I?' she said, tugging gently on his forelock. She smoothed the palm of her hand along his pricked ears until he tossed his head and trumpeted. She imagined he was part of the herd who were still out there somewhere on the pampas.

Biting back tears, she glanced towards the *hacienda.* Kruz would be showering down after his ride, she guessed. He would be washing away the dust of the day and, judging by his reaction to her news, he would be washing away all thoughts of Romy and their baby along with it.

CHAPTER ELEVEN

HE'D SLEPT ON it, and now he knew what he was going to do. Towelling down after his shower the next morning, he could see things clearly. Romy's news had stunned him. How could it not, considering his care where contraception was concerned? It shouldn't have happened, but now it *had* happened he would take control.

Tugging on a fresh pair of jeans and a clean top, he raked his thick dark hair into some semblance of order. The future of this baby was non-negotiable. He would not be a part-time parent. He knew the effect it had had on him when his parents had been killed. It wasn't Nacho's fault that Kruz had run wild, but he did believe that a child needed both its parents. Romy could have her freedom, and they would live independent lives, but she must move here to Argentina.

The internet was amazing, Romy concluded as she settled into her narrow seat on the commercial jet.

She'd used it to sell the images she didn't need to keep back for the Acosta charity, or for Grace, and had then used the proceeds to book her flight home. Alessandro had insisted on driving her to the airport and carrying her luggage as far as the check-in desk. He was a lovely man, sensitive enough not to ply her with questions. She didn't care that she wasn't flying home in style in a private jet. The staff in the cabin were polite and helpful, and before long she would be back in London on the brink of a new life.

As soon as she had taken the last shot she needed and made plans to leave Argentina she had known there would be no going back. This was the right decision—for her and for her child. She didn't need a man to help her raise her baby. She was strong and self-sufficient, she had her health, and she could earn enough money for both their needs. One thing was certain—she didn't need Kruz Acosta.

Really?

She had panicked to begin with, Romy reasoned as the big, wide jet soared high into the air. But making the break from Kruz was just what she needed. It was a major kick-start to the rest of her life. He was the one losing out if he didn't want to be part of this. She was fine with it. She could live man-free, as she had before.

Reaching for the headphones, she scrolled through the channels until she found a film she could lose herself in—or at least attempt to tune out the voice of her inner critic, who said that by turning her back on Kruz and leaving Argentina without telling him Romy had done the wrong thing yet again.

'Señorita Romily has gone,' Alessandro told him.

'What the hell do you mean, she's gone?' he demanded as Alessandro got out of the pick-up truck.

'She flew back to England this morning,' his elderly friend informed him, stretching his limbs. 'I just got back from taking her to the airport.' Alessandro levelled a challenging look at Kruz that said, *And what are you going to do about it?*

They didn't make men tame and accepting on the pampas, Kruz reflected as he met Alessandro's unflinching stare. 'She went back to England to *that* house?' he snarled, beside himself with fury.

Alessandro's shoulders lifted in a shrug. 'I don't know where she was going, exactly. "Back home" is all she told me. She talked of a lovely area by a canal in London while we were driving to the airport. She said I would love it, and that even so close to a city like London it was possible to find quiet places that are both picturesque and safe. She told me about the waterside cafés and the English pubs, and said there are plenty of places to push a pram.'

'She was stringing you along,' Kruz snapped impatiently. 'She guessed you wouldn't take her to the airport if you knew the truth about where she lived.' And when Alessandro flinched with concern at the thought that he might have led Romy into danger, Kruz lashed out with words as an injured wolf might howl in the night as the only way to express its agony. 'She lives in a terrible place, Alessandro. Even with all the operatives in my employ I cannot guarantee her safety there.'

'Then follow her,' his wise old friend advised.

Kruz shook his head, stubborn pride still ruling him. Romy was having his baby and she had left Argentina without telling him. Twisting the knife in the wound, his old friend Alessandro had helped Romy on her way. 'Why?' he demanded tensely, turning a blazing stare on his old friend's face. 'Why have you chosen to help her?

'I think you know why,' Alessandro said mildly.

'You think I'd hurt her?' he exclaimed with affront. 'You think because of everything that happened in the army I'm a danger to her?'

Alessandro looked sad. 'No,' he said quietly. 'You are the only one who thinks that. I helped Señorita Winner to go home because she's pregnant and because she needs peace now—not the anger you feel for yourself. Until you can accept that you have every right to a future, you have nothing to offer her. You have hurt her,' Alessandro said bluntly, 'and now it's up to you to make the first approach.'

'She didn't tell me she was pregnant.'

'Did you give her a chance?'

'I didn't know—'

'You didn't want to know. *I* knew,' Alessandro said quietly.

Kruz stood rigid for a moment, and then followed Alessandro to the stable, where he found the old *gaucho* preparing to groom his favourite horse.

'You drove her to the airport,' he said, still tight with indignation. '*Dios*, Alessandro, what were you thinking?'

When Alessandro didn't speak he was forced to master himself, and when he had done so he had to admit Alessandro was right. His old friend had done nothing wrong. This entire mess was of Kruz and Romy's making—mostly his.

'So she didn't tell you she was leaving?' Alessandro commented, still sweeping the grooming brush down his horse's side in rhythmical strokes.

'No, she didn't tell me,' he admitted. And why would she? He hadn't listened. He hadn't seen this coming. So the mother of his child had just upped and left the country without a word.

What now?

She wasn't *all* to blame for this, but one thing was certain. Romy might have pleased herself in the past, but now she was expecting his baby she would listen to *him*.

'No,' Romy said flatly, preparing to cut the line having refused Kruz's offer of financial help. 'And please don't call me at the office again.'

'Where the hell else am I supposed to call you?' he thundered. 'You never pick up. You can't keep on avoiding me, Romy.'

The irony of it, she thought. She knew they should meet to discuss the baby, but things had happened since she'd come back to England—big things—and now she was sick with loss and just didn't think she could take any more. Her mother had died. There—it was said…thought…so it must be true. It *was* true. She had arrived at the nursing home too late to see her mother alive. Somehow she had always imagined she would be there when the time came. The fact that her mother had slipped away peacefully in her sleep had done nothing to help ease her sense of guilt.

And none of it was Kruz's fault.

'Okay, let's meet,' she agreed, choosing an anonymous café on an anonymous road in the heart of the bustling metropolis. The café was close by both their offices, and with Kruz back in London the last thing she wanted was for them to bump into each other on the street.

'I could meet you at the house,' he said, 'if that's easier for you.'

There *was* no house. The lease was up. The house had gone. She was sleeping on a girlfriend's sofa until she found somewhere permanent.

'This can't be rushed, Romy,' Kruz remarked as

she was thinking things through. 'Five minutes of your time in a crowded café won't be enough.'

He was right. In a few months' time they would be parents. It still seemed incredible. It made her heart ache to be talking to him about such a monumental event that should affect them both equally while knowing they would never be closer than this. 'I'll make it a long lunch,' she offered.

She guessed she must have sounded patronising as Kruz repeated the address and cut the line.

Without him asking her to do so she had taken a DNA test to prove that the baby was his. She had had to do it before a solicitor would represent her. Putting everything in the hands of a stranger had felt like the final nail in the coffin containing their non-existent relationship. This meeting in the café with Kruz to sort out some of the practical aspects of parental custody was not much more.

Not much more? Did she really believe that? Just catching sight of Kruz through the steamed-up windows of the chic city centre café was enough to make her heart lurch. He'd already got a table, and was sipping coffee as he read the financial papers. He'd moved on with his life and so had she, Romy persuaded herself. She had suffered the loss of her mother while he'd been away—a fact she'd shared with no one. Kruz, of all people, would probably understand, but she wouldn't burden him with it. They weren't part of each other's lives in that way.

'Hey,' she murmured, dropping her bag on the seat by his side. 'Watch that for me, will you, while I get something to drink?'

Putting the newspaper down, he stood up. He stared at her without speaking for a moment. 'Let me,' he said at last, brushing past.

'No caffeine,' she called. 'And just an almond croissant, please.'

Just an almond croissant? Was that a craving or lack of funds?

He should have prepared himself for seeing Romy so obviously pregnant. He knew how far on she was, after all. He should have realised that the swell of her stomach would be more pronounced because she was so slender. If he had been prepared he might be able to control this feeling of being a frustrated protector who had effectively robbed himself of the chance to do his job.

Taking Romy's sparse lunch back to the table, he sat down. She played with the food and toyed with mint tea. *I hope you're eating properly,* he thought, watching her. There were dark circles beneath her eyes. She looked as if she wasn't sleeping. That made two of them.

'Let's get this over with,' he said, when she seemed lost in thought.

She glanced up and the focus of her navy blue eyes sharpened. 'Yes, let's get it over with,' she agreed. 'I've appointed a lawyer. I thought you'd find that easier than dealing with me directly—I know I will. I'm busy,' she said, as if that explained it.

'Business is good?' he asked carefully.

'You should know it is.' She glanced up, but her gaze quickly flickered away. 'Grace keeps me busy with the charity, and my work for that has led me on to all sorts of things.'

'That's good, isn't it?'

She smiled thinly.

'Are you still living at the same place?'

'Why do you ask?' she said defensively.

He should have remembered how combative Romy could be. He should have taken into account the fact that pregnancy hormones would accentuate this trait. But Romy's wellbeing and that of his child was his only concern now. He didn't want to fight with her. 'Just interested,' he said with a shrug.

'I don't need your money,' she said quickly. 'With money comes control, and I'm a free agent, Kruz.'

'Whoah…' He held his hands up. She was bristling to the point where he knew he had to pull her back somehow.

'I'd do anything for my child,' she went on, flashing him a warning look, 'but I won't be governed by your money and your influence. I don't need you, Kruz. I am completely capable of taking care of this.'

And completely hormonal, he supplied silently

as Romy's raised voice travelled, causing people to turn and stare.

'I'm not challenging your rights,' he said gently. 'This child has changed everything for both of us. Neither of us can remain isolated in own private world any longer, Romy.'

She had expected this meeting with Kruz to be difficult, but she hadn't expected to feel quite so emotional. This was torture. If only she could reach out instead of pushing him away.

The past was a merciless taskmaster, Romy concluded, for each time she thought about the possibility of a family unit, however loosely structured, she was catapulted back into that house where her mother had been little more than a slave to her father's much stronger will.

'You don't know anything about this,' she said distractedly, not even realising she was nursing her baby bump.

'I know quite a lot about it,' Kruz argued, which only made the ache of need inside her grow. 'I grew up on an *estancia* the size of a small city. I saw birth and death as part of the natural cycle of life. I saw the effect of pregnancy on women. So I do understand what you're going through now. And I know about your mother, Romy, and I'm very sorry for your loss.'

Kruz knew everything about everything. Of course he did. It was his business to know. 'Well, thank you for your insight,' she snapped, like a frightened little girl instead of the woman she had become.

Not all men were as principled as Kruz, but he would leave her to pick up the pieces eventually. Better she pushed him away now. It wasn't much of a plan, but it was all she'd got. She just hadn't expected it to be so hard to pull off.

'When the baby's born,' she said, straightening her back as she took refuge in practical matters, 'you will have full visiting rights.'

'That's very good of you,' Kruz remarked coldly.

She was being ridiculous. Kruz had the means to fight her through the courts until the end of time, while *her* resources were strictly limited. She might like to think she was in control, but that was a fantasy he was just humouring. 'Independence is important to me—'

'And to me too,' he assured her. 'But not at the expense of everyone around me.'

She was glad when he fell silent, because it stopped her retaliating and driving another wedge between them. 'I hope we can remain friends.'

'I'd say that's up to you,' he said, reaching for his jacket.

She wanted to say something—to reach out and touch him—but it had all gone wrong. 'I'll get the bill,' she offered, feeling she must do something.

Ignoring her, Kruz called the waitress over.

She wanted him in her life, but she couldn't live with the control that came with that. She felt like crying and banging her fists on the table with frustration. Only very reluctantly she accepted that those feelings were due to hormones. Her emotions were all over the place. She ached to share her hopes and fears about the baby with Kruz, and yet she was doing everything she could to drive him away.

'Ready to go?' he said, standing. 'My lawyers will be in touch with yours.'

'Great.'

This was it. This was the end. Everything was being brought to a close with a brusque statement that twisted in her heart like a knife. She got up too, and started to leave the table. But her belly got stuck. Kruz had to move the table for her. She felt so vulnerable. She couldn't pretend she didn't want to confide in him, share her fears with him. He stood back as she walked to the door. Somehow she managed to bang into someone's tray on one of the tables, and then she nearly sent a child flying when she turned around to see what she'd done.

'It's okay, I've got it,' Kruz said calmly, making sure everything was set to rights in his deft way, with his charisma and his smile.

'Sorry,' she said, feeling her cheeks fire up as she made her apologies to the people involved. They hardly seemed to notice her. They were so taken with Kruz. 'Sorry,' she said again when he joined her at the door. 'I'm so clumsy these days. When the baby's born we'll have another chat.'

He raised a brow at this and made no reply. Now he'd seen her he must think her ungainly and clumsy.

'I'll be in touch,' he said.

This was all happening too fast. The words wouldn't come out of her mouth quickly enough to stop him.

Pulling up the collar on his heavy jacket, he scanned the traffic and when he saw a gap dodged across the road.

Her heart was in shreds as her gaze followed him. She stayed where she was in the doorway of the café, sheltering in blasts of warm, coffee-scented air as customers arrived and left. When the door was opened and the chatter washed over her she began to wonder if a heart could break in public, while people were calling for their coffee or more ketchup on their chips.

Grace had taken her in, insisting Romy couldn't expect to keep healthy and look after her unborn child while she was sleeping on a friend's sofa. There was plenty of room in the penthouse, Grace had explained. Romy hadn't wanted to impose, but when Grace insisted that she'd welcome the company while Nacho was away on a polo tour Romy had given in. They could work together on the charity features while Romy waited for the birth of her child, Grace pointed out.

Romy had worked out that if she budgeted carefully she would have enough money to buy most of the things she needed for the baby in advance. She searched online to find bargains, and hunted tirelessly through thrift shops for the bigger items, but even with her spirit of make do and mend she couldn't resist a visit to Khalifa's department store when she noticed there was a sale on. She bought one adorable little suit at half-price but would have loved a dozen more, along with a soft blanket and a mobile to hang above the cot. But those, like the cuddly toys, were luxuries she had to pass up. The midwife at the hospital had given her a long list of essentials to buy before she gave birth.

Get over it, Romy told herself impatiently as her hormones got to work on her tear glands as she walked around the baby department. This baby was going to be born to a mother who adored it already and who would do anything for it.

A baby who would never know its grandmother and rarely see its father.

'Thanks a lot for that helpful comment,' she muttered out loud.

She could do without her inner pessimist. Emotional incontinence at this stage of pregnancy needed no encouragement. Leaning on the nearest cot, she foraged in her cluttered bag for a tissue to stem the flow of tears and ended up looking like a panda. Why did department stores have to have quite so many mirrors? So much for the cool, hard-edged photographer—she was a mess.

It had not been long since her mother's funeral, Romy reasoned as she took some steadying breaths. It had been a quiet affair, with just a few people from the care home. There was nothing sadder than an empty church, and she had felt bad because there had been no one else to invite. She felt bad now— *about everything*. Her ankles were swollen, her feet hurt, and her belly was weighing her down.

But she had a career she loved and prospects going forward, Romy told herself firmly as an assistant, noticing the state she was in, came over with a box of tissues.

'We see a lot of this in here,' the girl explained kindly. 'Don't worry about it.'

Romy took comfort from the fact that she wasn't the only pregnant woman falling to pieces during pregnancy—right up to the moment when the assistant added, 'Does the daddy know you're here? Shall I call him for you?' Only then did she notice Romy's ring-free hands. 'Oh, I'm sorry!' she exclaimed, slapping her hand over her mouth. 'I really didn't mean to make things worse for you.'

'You haven't,' Romy reassured her as a fresh flood of tears followed the first. She just wanted to be on her own so she could howl freely.

'Here—have some more tissues,' the girl insisted, thrusting a wad into Romy's hands. 'Would you like me to call you a cab?'

'Would you?' Romy managed to choke out.

'Of course. And I'll take you through the staff entrance,' the girl offered, leading the way.

Thank goodness Kruz couldn't see her like this—all bloated and blotchy, tear-stained and swollen, with her hair hanging in lank straggles round her face. Gone were the super-gelled spikes and kick-ass attitude, and in their place was…a baby.

He'd kept away from Romy, respecting her insistence that she was capable of handling things her way and that she would let him know when the baby was born. They lived in different countries, she had told him, and she didn't need his help. He was in London most of the time now, getting the new office up to speed, but he had learned not to argue with a pregnant woman. Thank goodness for Grace, who was still in London while Nacho was on a polo tour. At least she could reassure him that Romy was okay—though Grace had recently become unusually cagey about the details.

The irony of their situation wasn't lost on him, he accepted as he reversed into a space outside Khalifa's department store. He had pushed Romy away and now she was refusing to see him. She was about to give birth and he missed her. It was as simple as that.

But even though she refused his help there was nothing to say he couldn't buy a few things for their baby. Grace had said this was the best place to come—that Khalifa's carried a great range of baby goods.

The store also boasted the most enthusiastic assistants in London town, Kruz reflected wryly as they flocked around him. How the hell did he know what he wanted? He stood, thumbing his stubble, in the midst of a bewildering assortment of luxury goods for the child who must have everything.

'Just wrap it all up,' he said, eager to be gone from a place seemingly awash with happy couples.

'Everything, sir?' an assistant asked him.

'You know what a baby needs better than I do,' he pointed out. 'I'll take it all. Just charge it to my account.'

'And send it where, sir?'

He thought about the Acosta family's fabulous penthouse, and then his heart sank when he remembered Romy's tiny terrace on the wrong side of the tracks. He would respect her wish to say there for now, but after the birth…

The store manager, hurrying up at the sight of an important customer, distracted him briefly—but not enough to stop Kruz remembering that the only births he had attended so far were of the foals he owned, all of which had been born in the fabulous custom-built facility on the *estancia*.

No one owned Romy, he reflected as the manager continued to reassure him that Khalifa's could supply anything he might need. Romy was her own woman, and he had Grace's word for the fact that she would have the best of care during the birth of their baby at a renowned teaching hospital in the centre of London. But after the birth he suspected Romy would want to make her nest in that tiny terraced house.

Another idea occurred to him. 'Gift-wrap everything you think a newborn baby might need,' he instructed the manager, 'and have it made ready for collection.'

'Collection by van, sir?' The manager glanced around the vast, well-stocked floor.

'Yes,' Kruz confirmed. 'How long will that take?'

'At least two hours, plus loading time—'

He shrugged. 'Then I will return in two hours.'

Brilliant. Women loved surprises. He'd hire a van, load it up and deliver it himself.

The thought of seeing Romy again made him smile for the first time in too long. It would be good to see her shock when he rolled up with a van full of baby supplies. She would definitely unwind. Maybe they could even make a fresh start—as friends this time. Whatever the future held for them, he suspected they could both do with some down-time before the birth of their baby threw up a whole new raft of problems.

CHAPTER TWELVE

THAT WAS NOT a phantom pain.

Bent over double in the small guest cloakroom in the penthouse while Grace was at the shops buying something for their supper was not a good place to be…

Romy sighed with relief as the pain subsided. There was no cause for panic. If it got any worse she'd call an ambulance.

For once he didn't even mind the traffic because he was in such a good mood, and by the time he pulled the hired van outside the terraced house he was feeling better than positive. They would work something out. They both had issues and they both had to get over them. They had a baby to consider now.

Springing down from the van, he stowed the keys. Relying on Grace for snippets of information about Romy wasn't nearly good enough, but he was half to blame for allowing the situation to get this bad. Both he and Romy were always on the defensive.

always expecting to be let down. Raising his fist, he hammered on the door. Now he just had to hope she was in.

Oh, oh, oh... She had managed to crawl into the bathroom. *Emergency!*

They'd mentioned pressure at the antenatal classes, so she was hoping this was just a bit of pressure—

Pressure everywhere.

And no sign of Grace.

'Grace...' she called out weakly, only to have the silence of an empty apartment mock her. 'Grace, I need you,' she whimpered, knowing there was no one to hear her. 'Grace, I don't know what to do.'

Oh, for goodness' sake, pull yourself together! Of course you know what to do.

Now the pain had faded enough for her to think straight, maybe she did. Scrabbling about in her pockets, she hunted for her phone. All she had to do was dial the emergency number and tell them she was having a baby. What was so hard about that?

'Grace!' she exclaimed with relief, hearing the front door open. 'Grace? Is that you?'

'Romy?' Grace sounded as panicked as Romy felt. 'Romy, where are you?'

'On the floor in the bathroom.'

'On the floor—? Goodness—'

She heard Grace shutting her big old guide dog,

Buddy, in the kitchen before moving cautiously down the hall with her stick. 'Grace, I'm in here.' There were several bathrooms in the penthouse, and Grace would find her more easily if she followed the sound of Romy's voice.

'Are you okay?' Grace called out anxiously, trying to get her bearings.

That was a matter of opinion. 'I'm fine,' Romy managed, and then the door opened and Grace was standing there. Just having someone to share this with was a help.

Grace felt around with her stick. 'What on earth are you doing under the sink?'

'I had a little accident,' Romy admitted, chucking the towel she'd been using in the bath. 'Can't move,' she managed to grind out as another contraction hit her out of nowhere. 'Stay where you are, Grace. I don't want you slipping, or tripping over me—I'll be fine in a minute.'

'I'm calling for an ambulance,' Grace said decisively, pulling out her phone.

'Tell them my waters have broken and the baby's coming—and this baby isn't waiting for anything.'

'Okay, keep calm!' Grace exclaimed, sounding more panicked than Romy had ever heard her.

He had thoughts of reconciliation and an armful of Romy firmly fixed in his head as he hammered a second time on the door of the small terraced house.

Like before, the sound echoed and fell away. Shading his eyes, he peered through the window. It was hard to see anything through the voile the girls had hung to give them some privacy from the street. His spirits sank. His best guess…? The tenants of this house were long gone.

How could he not have known? He should have kept up surveillance—but if Romy had found out he was having her followed he would have lost her for good.

There was nothing more pitiful than a man standing outside an empty house with a heart full of hope and a van full of baby equipment. But he had to be sure. Glancing over his shoulder to check the street was deserted, he delved into the pocket of his jeans to pull out the everyday items that allowed him entry into most places. This, at least, was one thing he was good at.

The house was empty. Romy and her friends had packed up and gone for good. There were a few dead flowers in a milk bottle, as if the last person to turn out the lights hadn't been able to bear to throw them away and had given them one last drink of water.

That would be Romy. So where the hell was she?

Grace would know.

Grace had called the emergency services, and Romy was reassured to hear her friend's succinct instructions on how to access the penthouse with the code at the door so she wouldn't have to leave Romy's side. But the ambulance would have to negotiate the rush hour traffic, Romy realised, starting to worry again as her baby grew ever more insistent to enter the world. Even with sirens blaring the driver would face gridlock in this part of town.

She jumped as Grace's telephone rang. The sight of Grace's face was enough to tell her that the news was not good. 'Grace, what is it?'

'Nothing…'

But Grace's nervous laugh was less than reassuring. 'It must be something,' Romy insisted. 'What's happened, Grace?' She really hoped it wasn't bad news. She wasn't at her most comfortable with her head lodged beneath the sink.

'Seems the first ambulance can't get here for some reason,' Grace admitted. 'But they've told me not to worry as they're sending another—'

'Don't worry?' Romy exclaimed, then felt immediately guilty. Grace was doing everything she could. 'Can you ring them back and tell them I need someone right away? This baby won't wait.'

'I'll do that now,' Grace agreed, but the instant she started to dial her phone rang. 'Kruz?'

'No!' Romy exclaimed in dismay. 'I don't want to speak to him—there's no time to speak to him—' A contraction cut her off, leaving her panting for breath. By the time it had subsided Grace was off the phone. 'You'd better not have told him!' Romy exclaimed. 'Please tell me you didn't tell him. I couldn't bear for him to see me like this.'

'Too late. He's on his way.'

Romy groaned, and then wailed, 'I need to push!'

'Hold on—not yet,' Grace pleaded.

'I can't hold on!' She added a few colourful expletives. 'Sorry, Grace—didn't mean to shout at you—'

Kruz had heard some of this before Grace cut the line. He had called an ambulance too, but the streets were all blocked. It was rush hour, they'd told him—as if he didn't know that. Even using bus lanes and sirens the ambulance driver could only do the best he could.

'Well, for God's sake, *do* your best!' he yelled in desperation. And he never yelled. He had never lost his cool with anyone. *Other than where Romy and his child were concerned.*

The traffic was backed up half a mile away from where he needed to be. Pulling the van onto the pavement, he climbed out and began to run. Bursting into the penthouse, he followed the sound of Grace's voice to the guest cloakroom, where he found Romy wedged at an awkward angle between the sink and the door.

'Get off me,' she sobbed as he came to pick her up. 'I'm going to have a baby—'

As if he didn't know that! 'You're as weak as a kitten and you need to be strong for me, Romy,' he said firmly as he drew her limp, exhausted body into his arms. 'Grace, can you bring me all the clean towels you've got, some warm water and a cover for the baby. Do we have a cradle? Something to sponge Romy down? Ice if you've got it. Soft cloths and some water for her to sip.'

By this time he had shouldered his way into a bedroom, stripped the duvet away and laid Romy down across the width of the bed. He found a chair to support her legs. This was no time for niceties. He'd seen plenty of mares in labour and he knew the final stages. Romy's waters had broken in the cloakroom and now she was well past getting to the hospital in time.

'What are you doing?' she moaned as he started stripping off her clothes.

'You're planning to have a baby with your underwear on?'

'Stop it… Not you… I don't want you undressing me.'

'Well, Grace is busy collecting the stuff we're going to need,' he said reasonably. 'So if not me, who else do you suggest?'

'I don't want you seeing me like this—'

'Hard luck,' he said as she whimpered, carrying on with his job. 'Strong, Romy. I need strong, Romy. Don't go all floppy on me. I need you in fighting mode,' he said firmly, in a tone she couldn't ignore. 'This baby is ready to enter the world and it needs you to fight for it. This isn't about you and me any longer, Romy.'

As he was speaking he was making Romy as comfortable as he could.

'Are you listening to me, Romy?' Tenderly taking her tear-stained face between his hands, he watched with relief as her eyes cleared and the latest contraction subsided. 'That's better,' he whispered. And then, because he could, he brushed a kiss across her lips. 'We're going to do this together, Romy. You and me together,' he said, staring into her eyes. 'We're going to have a baby.'

'Mostly me,' she pointed out belligerently, and with a certain degree of sense.

'Yes, mostly you,' he confirmed. Then, seeing her eyes fill with apprehension again, he knelt on the floor at the side of the bed. 'But remember this,' he added, bringing her into his arms so he could will his strength into her, 'the harder you work, the sooner you'll be holding that baby in your arms. You've got to help him, Romy.'

'*Him?*'

'Or her,' he said, feeling a stab of guilt at the fact that he hadn't attended any of the scans or check-ups Romy had been to.

Yes, she'd asked him not to—but since when had he ever done anything he was told? Had she tamed the rebel? If she had, her timing was appalling. He should have been with her from the start. But this was not the best time to be analysing where their stubbornness had led them.

'Whether this baby is a boy or a girl,' he said, talking to Romy in the same calm voice he used with the horses, 'this is your first job as a mother. It's the first time your baby has asked you for help, so you have to get on it, Romy. You have to believe in your strength. And remember I'm going to be with you every step of the way.'

She pulled a funny face at that, and then she was lost to the next contraction. They were coming thick and fast now.

'How long in between?' he asked. 'Have you been keeping a check on things, Grace?' he asked Grace as she entered the room.

'Not really,' Grace admitted.

'Don't worry—you've brought everything I asked for. Could you put a cool cloth on Romy's head for me?'

'Of course,' Grace said, sounding relieved to be doing something useful as she felt her way around the situation in a hurry to do as he asked. 'I didn't realise it would all happen so quickly.'

'Neither did I,' Romy confessed ruefully, her voice muffled as she pressed her face into his chest.

'This is going really well,' he said, hoping he was right. 'It's not always this fast,' he guessed, 'but this is better for the baby.'

At least Romy seemed reassured as she braced

herself against him, which was all that mattered. The speed of this baby's arrival had surprised everyone—not least him.

'Grace, could you stay here with Romy while I scrub up?'

'No, don't leave me,' Romy moaned, clinging to him.

'You're going to be all right,' he said, gently detaching himself. 'Here, Grace—I'll pull up a chair for you.' Having made Romy comfortable on the bed, he steered Grace to the chair. 'Just talk to her,' he instructed quietly. 'Hold her hand until I get back.'

'Don't go,' Romy begged him again.

'Thirty seconds,' he promised.

'Too long,' she managed, before losing herself in panting again.

'My sentiments entirely,' he called back wryly from the bathroom door.

He was back in half that time. 'I'm going to take a look now.'

'You can't look!' Romy protested, sounding shocked.

Bearing in mind the intimacy they had shared, he found her protest endearing. 'I need to,' he explained. 'So please stop arguing with me and let's all concentrate on getting this baby safely into the world.'

'How many births have you attended?' Romy ground out as he got on with the job.

'More than you can imagine—and this one is going to be a piece of cake.'

'How can you know that?' she howled.

'Just two legs, and one hell of a lot smaller than my usual deliveries? Easy,' he promised, pulling back.

'How many human births?' she ground out.

'You'll be the first to benefit from my extensive experience,' he admitted, 'so you have the additional reassurance of knowing I'm fresh to the task.'

She wailed again at this.

'Just lie back and enjoy it,' he suggested. 'There's nowhere else we have to be. And with the next contraction I need you to push. Grace, this is where you come in. Let Romy grip your hands.'

'Right,' Grace said, sounding ready for action.

'I can see the head!' he confirmed, unable keep the excitement from his voice. 'Keep pushing, Romy. Push like you've never pushed before. Give me a slow count to ten, Grace. And, Romy? You push all the time Grace is counting. I'm going to deliver the shoulders now, so I need you to pant while I'm turning the baby slightly. That's it,' he said. 'One more push and you've got a baby.'

'*We've* got a baby,' Romy argued, puce with effort as she went for broke.

Romy's baby burst into the world with the same enthusiasm with which her parents embraced life. The infant girl didn't care if her parents were cool, or independent, or stubborn. All she asked for was life and food and love.

The paramedics walked in just as she was born. A scene of joy greeted them. Grace was standing back, clasping her hands in awe as the baby gave the first of many lusty screams, while Kruz was kneeling at the side of the bed, holding his daughter safely wrapped in a blanket as he passed her over to Romy. Grace had the presence of mind to ask one of the paramedics to record the moment on Romy's phone, and from then on it was all bustle and action as the medical professionals took over.

He could hardly believe it. They had a perfect little girl. A daughter. *His* daughter. His and Romy's daughter. He didn't need to wonder if he had ever felt like this before, because he knew he never had. Nothing he had experienced came close to the first sight of his baby daughter in Romy's arms, or the look on Romy's face as she stared into the pink screwed-up face of their infant child. The baby had a real pair of lungs on her, and could make as much noise as her mother and father combined. She would probably be just as stubborn and argumentative, he concluded, feeling elated. All thoughts of him and Romy not being ready for parenthood had vanished. Of course they were ready. He would defend this child with his life—as he would defend Romy.

Once the paramedics were sure that both mother and baby were in good health, they offered him a

pair of scissors to cut the cord. It was another inde-
scribable moment, and he was deeply conscious of
introducing another treasured life into the world.

'You've done well, sir,' one of the health professionals told him. 'You handled the birth beautifully.'

'Romy did that,' he said, unable to drag his gaze
away from her face.

Reaching for his hand, she squeezed it tightly.
'I couldn't have done any of this without you,' she
murmured.

'The first part, maybe,' he agreed wryly. 'But
after that I think you should get most of the praise.'

'Don't leave me!' she exclaimed, her stare fearful
and anxious on his face as they brought in a stretcher
to take Romy and their baby to hospital.

As soon as the paramedics had her settled he put
the baby in her arms. 'You don't get rid of me that
easily,' he whispered.

And for the first time in a long time she smiled.

CHAPTER THIRTEEN

SHE WOKE TO a new day, a new life. A life with her daughter in it, and—

'Kruz?'

She felt her anxiety mount as she stared around. *Where was he?* He must have slipped out for a moment. He must have been here all night while she'd been sleeping. She'd only fallen asleep on the understanding that Kruz stayed by her side.

Expecting to feel instantly recovered, she was alarmed to find her emotions were in a worse state than ever. She couldn't bear to lose him now. She couldn't bear to be parted from him for a moment. Especially now, after all he'd done for her. He'd been incredible, and she wanted to tell him so. She wanted to hold his hand and stare into his eyes and tell him with a look, with her heart, how much he meant to her. Kruz had delivered their baby. What closer bond could they have?

Hearing their daughter making suckling sounds in her sleep, she swung cautiously out of bed. Just picking up the warm little bundle was an incredible experience. The bump was now a real person. Staring down, she scrutinised every millimetre of the baby's adorable face. She had her father's olive skin, and right now dark blue eyes, though they might change to a compelling sepia like his in time. The tiny scrap even had a frosting of jet-black hair, with some adorable kiss curls softening her tiny face. The baby hair felt downy soft against her lips, and the scent of new baby was delicious—fresh and clean and powdered after the sponge-down she had been given in the hospital.

'And you have amazing eyelashes,' Romy murmured, 'exactly like your father.'

She looked up as a nurse entered the room. 'Have you seen Señor Acosta?' she asked.

'Mr Acosta left before dawn with the instruction that you were to have everything you wanted,' the nurse explained, with the type of dreamy look in her eyes Romy was used to where Kruz was concerned.

'He left?' she said, trying and failing to hide her unease. 'Did he say when he would be back?'

'All I've been told is that Mr Acosta's sister-in-law, Grace Acosta, will be along shortly to pick you up,' the nurse informed her.

Romy frowned. 'Are you *sure* he said that?'

'I believe your sister-in-law will be driven here.'

'Ah…' Romy breathed a sigh of relief, knowing Grace would laugh if she knew Romy's churning emotions had envisaged Grace trying to walk home with Romy at her side, carrying a newly delivered baby, and with a guide dog in tow.

A chauffeur-driven car!

This was another world, one Romy had tried so hard not to become caught up in—though she could hardly blame Grace for travelling in style. She should have thought this through properly long before now. She should have realised that having Kruz's baby would have repercussions far beyond the outline for going it alone she had sketched in her mind.

'The car will soon be here to take you and the baby back to the penthouse,' the nurse was explaining to her.

'Of course,' Romy said, acting as if she were reassured. She would have felt better if Kruz had been coming to pick them up, but that wouldn't happen because she had drawn up the rules to exclude him, so she could prove her independence and go it alone with her baby.

But he couldn't just walk away.

Could he?

She shook herself as the nurse walked back in.

'It was a wonderful birth—thanks to your partner. I bet you can't wait to start your new life together as a family.' The nurse stopped and looked at her, and then passed her some tissues without a word.

Like the assistant in the department store, the

nurse must have seen a lot of this, Romy guessed, scrubbing impatiently at her eyes. She was still trying to tell herself that Kruz had only gone to take a shower and grab a change of clothes when the nurse added some more information to her pot of woe.

'Mr Acosta said he had to fly as he had some urgent business to complete.'

'Fly?' Romy repeated. 'He actually said that? He said he had to *fly*?'

'Yes, that's exactly what he said,' the nurse confirmed gently. 'Get back into bed,' she added firmly as Romy started hunting for her clothes. 'You should be taking it easy. You've just given birth and the doctor hasn't discharged you yet.'

'I need my phone,' Romy insisted, padding barefoot round the room, collecting up her things.

So Kruz was just going to fly back to Argentina after delivering their baby? He was going to fly *somewhere*, anyway; the nurse had just said so. And she'd thought Kruz might have changed. The overload to her hormones could only be described as nuclear force meeting solar storm. She might just catch him before he took off, Romy concluded, trying to calm down when she found her phone.

'Mr Acosta did say you might want to take some pictures, so he had your camera couriered over.'

Of course he did, Romy thought, refusing to be placated.

The nurse gave her a shrewd and slightly amused

look as a frowning Romy began to stab numbers into her phone. 'I'll leave you to it,' she mouthed.

'Kruz?' Romy was speaking in a dangerously soft voice as the call connected. 'Is that you?'

'Of course it's me. Is something wrong?'

'Where are you? If you're still on the ground get back here right away—we need to talk.'

'Romy?'

She'd cut the line. He rang back. She'd turned her phone off.

With a vicious curse he slammed his fist down on the wheel. Starting the engine, he thrust the gears into Reverse and swung the Jeep round, heading back to the hospital at speed, with his world splintering into little pieces at the thought that something might have happened to Romy or their child.

'You were going to leave us!' Romy exclaimed the moment he walked back into the room.

'Don't you *ever* do that to me again,' he said. Ignoring her protests, he took Romy in his arms and hugged her tight.

'Do what?' she said in a muffled voice.

'Don't ever frighten me like that. I thought something had happened to you or the baby. Do you have any idea how much you mean to me?'

She stared into his eyes, disbelieving, until the force of his stare convinced her.

'If they hadn't told me at Reception that you were both well I don't know what I would have done.'

'Flown to Argentina?' she suggested.

'You can't seriously think I'd do that now?'

'The nurse said you had to fly.' Romy's mouth set in a stubborn line.

'I did have to fly—I had an appointment.'

'What were you doing? I know,' she said, stopping herself. 'Sorry—none of my business.'

'It's a long story,' Kruz agreed. 'Why don't I ring Grace and give her some warning before I take you back?'

'Good idea.' It was hard to be angry with Kruz when he looked like this, as he stared down at their child, but nothing had changed. This man was still Kruz Acosta—elusive, hard and driven. A man who did what he liked, when he liked. While she was still Romy Winner—self-proclaimed battle-axe and single mother.

'Well, that's settled,' Kruz said as he cut the line. 'Grace is going back to Argentina. Nacho is coming to collect her now, so you'll have the penthouse to yourself.'

She should be grateful for the short-term loan of such a beautiful home. 'Okay,' she said brightly, worrying about how she and the baby would rattle round the vast space.

'There's plenty of staff to help you,' Kruz pointed out.

'Great,' she agreed. The company of strangers

was just what she needed in her present mood. 'I'll get my things together.'

'Grace has organised everything for you, so there's nothing to worry about,' Kruz remarked as he leaned over the cradle.

She loved the way he cared about their baby, but she felt the first stirring of unease. Now the drama was over, would Kruz claim their daughter? He could provide so much more than she could for their child. Would it be selfish of her to cling on?

Of course not. There was no conflict. She kicked the rogue thought into touch. No one would part her from her baby. But would she be in constant conflict with Kruz for ever?

'You can't buy her,' she whispered, thinking out loud.

'*Buy* her?' Kruz queried with surprise. 'She's already mine.'

'Ours.'

'Romy, are you guilty of overreacting to every little comment I make, by any chance?' Before she could answer, Kruz pointed out that she *had* just given birth. 'Give yourself a break, Romy. I know how much your independence means to you, and I respect that. No one's going to take your baby away from you—least of all me.'

Biting her lip, she forced the tears back. Why did everything seem like a mountain to climb? 'I don't know what to think,' she admitted.

'Is this what I've been missing over the past few months?' Kruz asked wryly.

'I'm glad you think it's funny,' she said, knowing she *was* overreacting, but somehow unable to stop herself. 'Do you think you can house me in your glamorous penthouse and pull my strings from a distance?'

'Romy,' Kruz said with a patient sigh, 'I could never think of you as a puppet. Your strings would be permanently tangled. And if we're going to sort out arrangements for the future I don't want to be doing it in a hospital. Do you?'

She flashed a look at him. Kruz's gaze was steady, but those arrangements for the future he was talking about meant they would part.

Count to ten, she counselled herself. *Right now you're viewing everything through a baby-lens.*

She slowly calmed down—enough to pick up her camera. 'Just one shot of you and the baby,' she said.

'Why don't we ask the nurse if she'll take one of all three of us together?' Kruz suggested. 'There will never be another moment like this as we celebrate the birth of our beautiful daughter.'

'You're right,' Romy agreed quietly. 'I feel like such a fool.'

'No,' Kruz argued. 'You feel like every new mother—full of hope and fear and excitement and doubt. You're exhausted and wondering if you can cope. And I'm telling you as a close observer of Romy Winner that you can. And what's more you look pretty good to me,' he added, sending her a look that made her breath hitch.

She hesitated, not knowing whether to believe him as the nurse came in to take the shot. 'Do I look okay?' she asked, suddenly filled with horror at the thought of ruining the photo of gorgeous Kruz and his beautiful daughter—and her.

'Take the baby,' he said, putting their little girl in her arms. 'You look great. I like your hair silky and floppy,' he insisted, 'and I like your unmade-up face. But if you want gel spikes and red tips, along with tattoos in unusual places and big, black Goth eyes, that's fine by me too.'

'You're being unusually understanding,' Romy commented, trying to make a joke of it. Once a judgement was made regarding their daughter's future they would be parents, not partners, and she should never get the two mixed up.

'I'm undergoing something of an emotional upheaval myself,' Kruz confessed, putting his arm loosely around her shoulders for the happy family shot. 'I guess having a child changes you...' His voice trailed off, but his tender look spoke volumes as he glanced down at their daughter, sleeping soundly in Romy's arms.

'I've never seen you like this before,' Romy commented as Kruz straightened up.

Kruz said nothing.

'So, will you be going back to Argentina as soon as everything's settled here?' she pressed as the nurse took the baby from her and handed her to Kruz.

'I'm in no hurry,' Kruz murmured, staring intently at his daughter.

This was a *very* different side of Kruz, Romy realised, deeply conscious of his depth of feeling as she checked she had packed everything ready for leaving. He was oblivious to everything but his daughter, and that frightened her. *Would* he try to take her baby from her?

His overriding concern was that his child should grow up as part of a strong family unit as he had—thanks to Nacho. But Romy must make her own decisions and he would give her time.

'Are we ready?' he said briskly, once Romy was seated in the wheelchair in which hospital policy insisted she must be taken outside.

'Yes, I'm ready,' Romy confirmed, her gaze instantly locking onto their baby as he placed their daughter in her arms.

'Then let's go.' He was surprised by his eagerness to leave the hospital so he could begin his new life as a father. He couldn't wait to leave this sterile environment where no expressions of intimacy or emotion were possible. He longed to relax, so he could express his feelings openly.

'Kruz—'

'What?' he said, wondering if there was any more
affecting sight than a woman holding her newborn
child.

Romy shook her head and dropped her gaze.
'Nothing,' she said.

'It must be something.' She was exhausted, he
realised, coming to kneel by her side. 'What is it?'
he prompted as the nurse discreetly left the room.

'I'm just…' She shook her head, as new to the
expression of emotion as he was, he guessed. And
then she firmed her jaw and looked straight at him.
'I'm just worrying about the effect of you walking
in and out of our baby's life.'

'Don't look for trouble, Romy.'

Why not? her look seemed to say. He blamed
the past for Romy's concerns. He blamed the past
for his inability to form close relationships outside
his immediate family. He guessed that the birth of
this child had been a revelation for both of them. It
wasn't a case of daring to love, but trying not to—if
you dared. Hostage for life, he thought, staring into
his daughter's eyes, and a willing one. This wealth
of feeling was something both he and Romy would
have to get used to and it would take time.

'Don't push me away just yet,' he said, sounding
light whilst inwardly he was painfully aware of how
much they both stood to lose if they handled this

badly. 'I've done as you asked so far, Romy. I've kept my distance for the whole of your pregnancy, so grant me a little credit. But please don't ask me to keep my distance from my child, because that's one thing I can't do.'

'I thought you didn't want commitment,' she said.

He wanted to say, *That was then and this is now,* but he wasn't going to say anything before he was ready. He wouldn't mislead Romy in any way. He had to be sure. From a life of self-imposed isolation to this was quite a leap, and the feelings were all new to him. He wanted them to settle, so he could be cool and detached like in the old days, when he'd been able to think clearly and had always known the right thing to do.

'Grace said you've never shared your life with anyone,' she went on, still fretting.

'People change, Romy. Life changes them.'

He sprang up as the nurse returned. This wasn't the time for deep discussions. Romy had just had a baby. Her hormones were raging and her feelings were all over the place.

'Time to go,' the nurse announced with practised cheerfulness, taking charge of Romy's chair.

While the nurse was wrapping a blanket around Romy's knees and making sure the baby was warmly covered, Romy turned to him. Grabbing hold of his wrist, she made him look at her. 'So what do you want?' she asked him.

'I want to forget,' he said, so quietly it was almost a thought spoken out loud.

CHAPTER FOURTEEN

ROMY REMAINED SILENT during the journey to the penthouse. She was thinking about Kruz's words.

What did he want to forget? His time in the Special Forces, obviously. Charlie had given her the clue there. Charlie had said Kruz was a hero, but Kruz clearly didn't believe his actions could be validated by the opinion of his peers. Medals were probably just pieces of metal to him, while painful memories were all too vivid and real. She couldn't imagine there was much Kruz couldn't handle—but then she hadn't been there, hadn't seen what he'd seen or been compelled to do what he had done. She only knew him as a source of solid strength, as his men must have known him, and her heart ached to think of him in torment.

'Are you okay?' he said, glancing at her through the mirror.

'Yes,' she said softly. *But I'm worried about you... so worried about you.*

Everything had been centred around her and the

baby, and that was understandable given the circumstances, but who was caring for Kruz? She wanted to…so badly; if only he'd let her. There were times for being a warrior woman and times when just staring into the face of their baby daughter and knowing Kruz was close by, like a sentinel protecting them, was enough. Knowing they were both safe because of him had given her the sort of freedom she had never had before—odd when she had always imagined close relationships must be confining. He'd given her that freedom. He'd given her so much and now she wanted to help him.

He wasn't hers to help, she realised as Kruz glanced at her again through the driving mirror. She mustn't be greedy. But that was easier said than done when his eyes were so warm and so full of concern for her.

'My driving okay for you?'

As he asked the question she laughed. Kruz was driving like a chauffeur—smoothly and avoiding all the bumps. The impatient, fiery polo-player was nowhere to be seen.

'You're doing just fine,' she said, teasing him in a mock-serious tone. 'I'll let you know if anything changes.'

'You do that,' he said, his eyes crinkling in the mirror. 'You must be tired,' he added.

'And elated.' And worried about the future…and most worried of all about Kruz. They had no future

together—none they'd talked about, anyway—and
what would happen to him in the future? Would he
spend his whole life denying himself the chance of
happiness because of what had happened in the past?

She pulled herself together, knowing she couldn't
let anything spoil this homecoming when Grace and
Kruz had gone to so much trouble for her.

'I'm looking forward so much to seeing Grace,'
she said, 'and being on familiar ground instead of
in the hospital. It makes everything seem...' She really was lost for words.

'Exciting,' Kruz supplied.

Her eyes cleared as she stared into his through the
mirror. 'Yes, exciting,' she agreed softly.

'I can understand that. Grace has been rushing
around like crazy to get things ready in time. She's
as excited as we are.'

We? He made them sound like a couple...

It was just a figure of speech, Romy reminded
herself, though Kruz was right about life changing
people. They had both been cold and afraid to show
their feelings until the baby arrived, but now it was
hard to hide their feelings. She'd been utterly determined to go it alone after the birth of their child.
The baby had changed her. The baby had changed
them both. She couldn't be more thrilled that Kruz
would be sharing this homecoming with her.

She gazed at the back of his head, loving every
inch of him—his thick dark hair, waving in disor-

der, and those shoulders broad enough to hoist an ox. She loved this man. She loved him with every fibre in her being and only wanted him to be happy. But first Kruz had to relearn how to enjoy life without feeling guilty because so many of his comrades were dead. She understood that now.

She had so much to be grateful for, Romy reflected as Kruz drove smoothly on. As well as meeting Kruz, and the birth of their beautiful daughter, these past few months had brought her some incredible friendships. Charlie and Alessandro—and Grace, who was more of a sister than a friend.

And Kruz.

Always Kruz.

Her heart ached with longing for him.

'Grace has been working flat out with the housekeeper to get the nursery ready,' he revealed, bringing her back to full attention.

'But I won't be staying long,' she blurted, suddenly frightened of falling into this seductive way of life when it wasn't truly hers. And Kruz wasn't her man—not really.

'We both wanted to do this for you,' Kruz insisted. 'The penthouse is your home for as long as you want it to be, Romy. You do know that, don't you?'

'Yes.' Like a lodger.

She couldn't say anything more. Her feelings were so mixed up. She was grateful—of course she was grateful—but she was still clinging to the illusion that somehow, some day, they could be a proper family. And that was just foolish. Now tears were stabbing the backs of her eyes again. Pressing her lips together, she willed herself to stop the flow. Kruz had enough on his plate without her blubbing all the time.

'I really appreciate everything you've done,' she said when she was calmer. 'It's just—'

'You don't want to feel caged,' he supplied. 'You're proud and you want to do things your way. I think I get that, Romy.'

There was an edge to his voice that told her he felt shut out. Maybe there was no solution to this— maybe she just had to accept that and move on. She could see she was pushing him away, but it was only because she didn't know what else to do without appearing to take too much for granted.

'You're very kind to let me stay at the penthouse,' she said, realising even as she spoke that she had made herself sound more like a grateful lodger thanking her landlord than ever.

Kruz didn't appear to notice, thank goodness, and as he pulled the limousine into the driveway of the Acosta family's Palladian mansion he said, 'And now you can get some well-earned rest. I'm determined you're going to be spoiled a little, so enjoy it while you can. Stay there—I'm coming round to help you out.'

She gazed out of the window as she waited for Kruz to open the door. The Acosta family owned the whole of this stately building, which was to be her home for the next few weeks. Divided into gracious apartments, it was the sort of house she would never quite get used to entering by the front door, she realised with amusement.

'This isn't a time for independence, Romy,' Kruz said, seeing her looking as he opened the door. 'You'll be happy here—and safe. And I want you to promise me that you'll let Grace look after you while she's here. It might only be for a few more days, but it's important for Grace too. She's proving something to herself—I think you know that.'

That her blind friend could have children and care for them as well as any other mother? Yes, she knew that. The fact that Kruz knew too proved how much they'd both changed.

'Grace has been longing for this moment,' he went on. 'Everyone has been longing for this moment,' he added, taking their tiny daughter out of her arms with the utmost care.

She would have to get used to this, Romy told herself wryly as Kruz closed her door and moved round to the back of the vehicle. But not too much, she thought, gazing up at the grand old white building in front of them. This sort of life—this sort of house—was the polar opposite of what she could afford.

Every doubt she had was swept away the moment she walked inside the penthouse and saw Grace and the staff waiting to welcome her, and when she saw what they'd done, all the trouble Grace had gone to, she was instantly overwhelmed and tearful. They had transformed one of the larger bedroom suites into the most beautiful nursery, with a bathroom off.

'Thank you,' she said softly, walking back to Grace, who was standing in the doorway with her guide dog, Buddy. Touching Grace's arm, Romy whispered, 'I can't believe you've done all this for me.'

'It's for Kruz as well as for you,' Grace said gently. 'And for your baby,' she added, reaching out to find Romy and give her a hug. 'I wanted you to come home to something special for you and your new family, Romy.'

If only, Romy thought, glancing at Kruz. They weren't a proper family—not really. Kruz was doing this because he felt he should—because he was a highly principled man of duty and always had been.

Kruz caught her looking at him and stared back, so she nodded her head, smiling in a way she hoped would show him how much she appreciated everything he and Grace had done for her, whilst at the same time reassuring him that she didn't expect him to devote the rest of his life to looking out for her.

She felt even more emotional when she put their tiny daughter into the beautifully carved wooden crib. Grace had dressed it with the finest Swiss lace, and the lace was so delicate she could imagine Grace selecting this particular fabric by touch. The thought moved her immeasurably. She wanted to hug Grace so hard neither of them could breathe. She wanted to tell Grace that having friends like her made her glad to be alive. She wanted to tell her that, having been so determined to go it alone, she was happy to be wrong. She wanted to be able to express her true feelings for Kruz, to let him know how much he meant to her. But she had to remind herself that they had agreed to do this as individuals, each of them taking a full part in their daughter's life, but separately, and she couldn't go back on her word.

Damn those pregnancy hormones!

The tears were back.

How could anyone who had been such a fearless reporter, a fearless woman, be reduced to this snivelling mess? When it came to being a woman in love, she was lost, Romy realised as Grace explained that the housekeeper had helped her to put everything in place. Romy was only too glad to be called back from the brink by practical matters as Grace went on to explain that she had also hired a night nurse, so that Romy could get some rest.

'I hope you don't mind me interfering?'

'Of course not,' Romy said quickly. 'It isn't interfering. It's kindness. I can't thank you enough for all you've done.'

'You're crying?' Grace asked her with surprise when she broke off.

Grace could hear everything in a voice, Romy remembered, knowing how Grace's other senses had leapt in to compensate for her sight loss. 'Everything makes me cry right now,' she admitted. 'Hormones,' she added ruefully, conscious that Kruz was listening. 'I've been an emotional train wreck since the birth.'

She seemed to have got away with it, Romy thought as Grace and the nurse took over. Or maybe Grace was just too savvy to probe deeper into her words, and the nurse was too polite. Kruz seemed unconcerned—though he did suggest she take a break. Remembering his words about Grace wanting to help, she was quick to agree.

'Champagne?' he suggested, leading the way into the kitchen. Her heart felt too big for her chest just watching him finding glasses, opening bottles, squeezing oranges.

'What you've done for me—' Knowing if she went on she'd start crying again, she steeled herself, because there were some things that had to be said. 'What you've done for our baby—the way you helped me during the birth—'

'It was a privilege,' Kruz said quietly.

Her cheeks fired red as he stared at her. She didn't know what he expected of her. There was so much she wanted to say to him, but he had turned away.

'Drink your vitamins,' he said, handing her the perfect Buck's Fizz.

'Thanks…' She didn't look at him. Was she supposed to act as if they were just friends? How was she supposed to act like a rational human being where Kruz was involved? How could she close her heart to this man? Having Kruz deliver their baby had brought them closer than ever.

'You're very thoughtful,' he said as he topped up her glass with the freshly squeezed juice.

'I was just thinking we almost had something…' Her face took on a look of horror as she realised what she'd said. Her wistful thoughts had poured out in words.

'And now it's over?' he said.

'And now it can never be the same,' she said, making a dismissive gesture with her hand, as if all those feelings inside her had been nothing more than a passing whim.

Kruz made no comment on this. Instead he said, 'Shall we raise a glass to our daughter?'

Yes, that was something they could both do safely. And they *should* rejoice. This was a special day. 'Our daughter, who really should have a name,' she said.

'Well, you've had a few months to think about it,' Kruz pointed out. 'What ideas have you had?'

'I didn't want to decide without—' She stopped, and then settled for the truth. 'I didn't want to decide without consulting you, but I thought Elizabeth... after my mother.'

Kruz's lips pressed down with approval. 'Good idea. I've always liked the name Beth. But what about you, Romy?' he said, coming to sit beside her.

'What about me?'

She stared into her glass as if the secret of life was locked in there. There was only one place she wanted to be, and that was right here with this man. There was only one person she wanted to be, and that was Romy Winner—mother, photographer and one half of this team.

'Come on,' Kruz prompted her. 'What do you want for the future? Or is it too early to ask?'

A horrible feeling swept over her—a suspicion, really, that Kruz was about to offer to fund whatever business venture she had in mind. 'I can't see further than now.'

'That's understandable,' he agreed. 'I just wondered if you had any ideas?'

She looked at him in bewilderment as he moved to take the glass out of her hand, and only then realised that she'd been twisting it and twisting it. She gave it up to him, and asked, 'What about you? What do *you* want, Kruz?'

'Me?' He paused and gave a long sigh, rounded off with one of those careless half-smiles he was so good at when he wanted to hide his true feelings.

'I have things to work through, Romy,' he said, his eyes turning cold.

Was this Kruz's way of saying goodbye? A chill ran through her at the thought that it might be.

For what seemed like an eternity neither of them spoke. She clung to the silence like a friend, because when he wasn't speaking and they were still sitting together like this she could pretend that nothing would change and they would always be close.

'I've seen a lot of things, Romy.'

She jerked alert as he spoke, wondering if maybe, just maybe, Kruz was going to give her the chance to help him break out of his self-imposed prison of silence. 'When you were in the army?' she guessed, prompting him.

'Let's just say I'm not the best of sleeping partners.'

He was already closing off. 'Do you have nightmares?' she pressed, feeling it was now or never if she was going to get through to him.

'I have nightmares,' Kruz confirmed.

They hadn't done a lot of sleeping together, so she wouldn't know about them, Romy realised, cursing her lust for him. She should have spent more time getting to know him. It was easy to be wise after the event, she thought as Kruz started to tell her something else—something that surprised her.

'I'm going to move in downstairs,' he said. 'There's

an apartment going begging and I want to see my daughter every day.'

Part of her rejoiced at this, while another part of her felt cut out—cut off. To have Kruz living so close by—to see him every day and yet know they would never be together...

'It's better this way,' he said, drawing her full attention again. 'I'm hard to live with, Romy, and impossible to sleep with. And you need your rest, so this is the perfect solution.'

'Yes,' she said, struggling to convince herself. If Kruz was suffering she had to help him. 'Maybe if you could confide in someone—'

'You?'

She realised how ridiculous that must sound to him and her face flamed red. Romy Winner, hard-nosed photojournalist, reduced not just to a sappy, hormonal mess but to a woman who couldn't even step up to the plate and say: *Yes, me. I'm going to do it.* 'I'll try, if you'll give me the chance,' she said instead.

Pressing his lips together, Kruz shook his head. 'It's not that easy, Romy.'

'I didn't expect it would be. I just think that when you've saved so many lives—'

'Someone should save *me*?' He gave a laugh without much humour in it. 'It doesn't work that way.'

'Why not?' she asked fiercely.

'Because I've done things I'll never be able to

forget,' he said quietly, and when he looked at her this time there was an expression in his eyes that said: *Just drop it.*

But she never could take good advice. 'Healing is a long process.'

'A lifetime?'

Kruz's face had turned hard, but it changed just as suddenly and gentled, as if he was remembering that she had recently given birth. 'You shouldn't be thinking about any of this, Romy. Today is a happy day and I don't want to spoil it for you.'

'Nothing you could say would spoil it,' she protested, wanting to add that she could never be truly happy until Kruz was too. But that would put unfair pressure on him. She sipped her drink to keep her mouth busy, wondering how two such prickly, complicated people had ever found each other.

'Believe me, you should be glad I'm keeping my distance,' Kruz said as he freshened their drinks. 'But if you need me I'm only downstairs.'

And that was a fact rather than an invitation, she thought—a thought borne out as Kruz stood up and moved towards the door. 'I have to go now.'

'Go?' The shock in her voice was all too obvious.

'I have business to attend to,' he explained.

'Of course.' And Kruz's business wasn't her business. What had she imagined? That he was going to pull her into his arms and tell her that everything would be all right—that the past could be brushed aside, just like that?

He stopped with his hand on the door. 'You believe in the absolution of time, Romy, but I'm still looking for answers.'

She couldn't stop him leaving, and she knew that Kruz could only replace his nightmares when something that made him truly happy had taken their place.

'It's good that you'll be living close by so you can see Beth,' she said. Perhaps that would be the answer. She really hoped so.

Kruz didn't answer. He didn't turn to look at her. He didn't say another word. He just opened the door and walked through it, shutting it quietly behind him, leaving her alone in the kitchen, wondering where life went from here. One step at a time, she thought, one step at a time.

She couldn't fault him as a devoted father. Kruz spent every spare moment he had with Beth. But where Romy was concerned he was distant and enigmatic. This had been going on for weeks now, and she missed him. She missed his company. She missed his warm gaze on her face. She missed his solid presence and his little kindnesses that gave her an opening to reach in to his world and pay him back with some small, silly thing of her own.

Grace had returned to Argentina with Nacho—

though they were expected back in London any day soon. This was a concern for Romy, as she knew Grace had hoped a relationship might develop between Romy and Kruz. It was going to be a little bit awkward, explaining why Romy's new routine involved Beth, mother and baby groups, and learning to live life as a single mother, while the father of her baby lived downstairs.

Kruz had issues to work through, and she understood that, but she wished he'd let her help him. She had broached the subject on a few occasions, but he'd brushed her off and she'd drawn back, knowing there was nothing she could say if he wouldn't open up.

The day after Nacho and Grace arrived back in London, Kruz dropped by with some flowers he'd picked up from the market. 'I got up early and I felt like buying all you girls some flowers,' he said, before breezing out again.

This was nice—this was good, Romy told herself firmly as she arranged the colourful spray in a glittering crystal vase. She felt good about herself, and about her life here in Acosta heaven. She was already taking photographs with thoughts of compiling a book. She treasured every moment she spent with her baby. And watching Kruz with Beth was the best.

Crossing to the window, she smiled as she watched him pace up and down the garden, apparently deep in conversation with their daughter. She longed to be part of it—part of them—part of a family that was three instead of two. But she had to stick to the unofficial rules she'd drawn up—rules that allowed Romy to get on with her life independently of Kruz. They both knew that at some point she would leave and move into rented accommodation, and when she did that Kruz had promised to set up an allowance for Beth, knowing very well that Romy would never take money for herself.

As if the money mattered. Her eyes welled up at the thought of parting from Kruz. What if she moved to the other side of London and never saw him again except when he came to collect Beth? When had such independence held any allure? She couldn't remember when, or what that fierce determination to go it alone had felt like. Independence at all costs was no freedom at all.

This wasn't nice—this wasn't good. Sitting down, she buried her face in her hands, wishing her mother were still alive so they could talk things through as they'd used to before her father had damaged her mother's mind beyond repair. Angry with herself, she sprang up again. She was a mother, and this was no time for self-indulgence. It was all about Beth now.

She was used to getting out there and looking after herself. No wonder she was frustrated, Romy reasoned. In fairness, Kruz had suggested that a babysitter should come in now and then, so Romy could gradually return to doing more of the work she loved. She had resigned from *ROCK!*, of course, but even Ronald, her picture editor, had said she shouldn't waste her talent.

She started as the phone rang and went to answer it.

'I'm bringing Beth up.'

'Oh, okay.' She sounded casual, but in her present mood she might just cling to him like an idiot when he arrived, and burst into tears.

No. She would reassure him by pulling herself together and carrying on alone with Beth as she had always planned to do; anything less than that would be an insult to her love for Kruz.

He bumped into Nacho and Grace on his way back into the house. They were staying in the garden apartment on the ground floor, to ensure they had some privacy. It was a good arrangement, this house in London. Big enough for the whole Acosta family, it had been designed so each of them had their own space.

Nacho asked him in for a drink. Grace declined to join them, saying she would rather play with Beth while she had the chance, but he got the feeling, as Grace took charge of the stroller, that his brother's wife was giving them some time alone.

'You've made a great marriage,' he observed as

Grace, her guide dog, Buddy, and baby Beth made their way along the hallway to the master suite.

'Don't I know it?' his brother murmured, gazing after his bride.

As he followed Nacho's stare he realised that for the first time in a long time he felt like a full member of the family again, rather than a ghost at the feast. It was great to see Nacho and to be able to share all his news about Romy and their daughter, and how being present at the birth of Beth had made him feel.

'Like there's hope for me,' he said, when Nacho pressed him for more.

'You've always been too hard on yourself,' Nacho observed, leading the way into the drawing room. 'And a lifetime of self-denial changes nothing, my brother.'

Coming from someone whose thoughts he respected, those straight-talking words from his brother hit home. It made him want to draw Romy and Beth together into a family—*his* family.

'Have you told Romy how you feel about her?' Nacho said.

'How I...?' Years of denying his feelings prompted him to deny it, but Nacho knew him too well, so he shrugged instead, admitting, 'I bought her some flowers today.'

'Instead of talking to her?'

'I talk.'

Nacho looked up from the newspaper he'd been scanning on the table.

'You talk?' he said. 'Hello? Goodbye?'

They exchanged a look.

'I'm going to find my wife,' Nacho told him, and on his way across the room he added, 'Babies change quickly, Kruz.'

'In five minutes, brother?'

'You know what I mean. Romy will move out soon. We both know it. She's not the type of woman to wait and see what's going to happen next. She'll make the move.'

'She won't take Beth away from me.'

'You have to make sure of that.'

'We live cheek by jowl already.'

'What?' Nacho scoffed, pausing by the door. 'You live downstairs—she lives upstairs with the baby. Is that what you want out of life?'

'It seems to be what Romy wants.'

'Then if you love her change her mind. Or I'll tell you what will happen in the future. You'll pass Beth between you like a ping-pong ball because both of you stood on your pride. You're not in the army now, Kruz. You're not part of that tight world. *You* make the rules.'

Kruz was still reeling when Nacho left the room. His brother had made him face the truth. He had returned to civilian life afraid to love in case he jinxed that person. He had discarded his feelings in order to protect others as he had tried to protect his men. By the time Romy turned his world on its head he hadn't even been in recovery. But she had started the process, he realised now, and there was no turning back.

The birth of Beth had accelerated everything. The nightmares had stopped. He looked forward to every day. Every moment of every day was precious and worthwhile now Romy and Beth were part of his life. That was what Romy had given him. She had given him love to a degree where not allowing himself to love her back was a bigger risk to his sanity than remembering everything in the past that had brought him to this point.

Nacho was right. He should tell Romy what she'd done for him and how he felt about her. Better still, he should show her.

CHAPTER FIFTEEN

WHEN KRUZ CALLED to explain to Romy that he and Beth were down with Grace and Nacho, so she didn't worry about Beth, he added that he wanted to take her somewhere and show her something.

She fell apart. Not crying. She was over that. Her hormones seemed to have settled at last. It was at Kruz's suggestion that Nacho and Grace should look after Beth while he took Romy out. Take her out without Beth as a buffer between them? She wasn't ready for that.

She would never be ready for that.

Her heart started racing as she heard the strand of tension in his voice that said Kruz was fired up about something. Whatever this something was, it had to be big. There was only one thing she could think of that fired the Acosta boys outside the bedroom. And the bedroom was definitely off the agenda today. In fact the bedroom hadn't been on the agenda for quite some time.

And whose fault was that?

Okay, so she'd been confused—and sore for a while after Beth's birth.

And now?

Not so sore. But still confused.

'Is it a new polo pony you want me to see?' she asked, her heart flapping wildly in her chest at the thought of being one to one with him.

'No,' Kruz said impatiently, as if that was the furthest thing from his mind. 'I just need your opinion on something. Why all the questions, Romy? Do you want to come or not?'

'Wellies, jeans and mac?' she said patiently. 'Or smart office wear?'

'You have some?'

'Stop laughing at me,' she warned.

'Those leggings and flat boots you used wear around *ROCK!* will do just fine. Ten minutes?'

'Do you want a coffee before we go—?' Kruz was in a rush, she concluded as the line was disconnected.

Ten minutes and counting and she had discarded as many outfits before reverting reluctantly to Kruz's suggestion. It was the best idea, but that didn't mean that following anyone's suggestions but her own came easily to her. Her hair had grown much longer, so she tied it back. She didn't want to look as if she was trying too hard.

What would they talk about…?

Beth, of course, Romy concluded, adding some

lips gloss to her stubborn mouth. And a touch of grey eyeshadow… And just a flick of mascara… Oh, and a spritz of scent. That really was it now. She'd make coffee to take her mind off his arrival—and when he did arrive she would sip demurely, as if she didn't have a care in the world.

While she was waiting for the coffee to brew she studied some pictures that had been taken of Kruz at a recent polo match. *She* would have done better. She would have taken him in warrior mode—restless, energetic and frustratingly sexy.

While she was restless, energetic and *frustrated*, Romy concluded wryly, leaning back in her chair.

She leapt to her feet when the doorbell rang, feeling flushed and guilty, with her head full of erotic thoughts. Kruz had his own key, but while she was staying at the penthouse he always rang first. It was a little gesture that said Kruz respected her privacy. She liked that. Why pretend? She liked everything about him.

She had to force herself to take tiny little steps on her way to the door.

Would she ever get used to the sight of this man?

As Kruz walked past her into the room he filled the space with an explosion of light. It was like having an energy source standing in front of her. Even dressed in heavy London clothes—jeans, boots, jacket with the collar pulled up—he was all muscle and tan: an incredible sight. *You look amazing,* she thought as he swept her into his arms for a disappointingly chaste kiss. Was it possible to die of frustration? If so, she was well on her way.

'I've missed you,' he said, pulling her by the hand into the kitchen. 'Do I smell coffee? Are you free for the rest of the day?'

'So many questions,' she teased him, exhaling with shock as he swung her in front of him. 'I have *some* free time,' she admitted cautiously, suddenly feeling unaccountably shy. 'Why?'

'Because I'm excited,' Kruz admitted. 'Can't you tell?'

Pressing her lips down, she pretended she couldn't.

He laughed.

Her heart was going crazy. Were they teasing each other now?

'There's something I really want to show you,' he said, turning serious.

'Okay…' She kept her expression neutral as Kruz dropped his hands from her arms. She still didn't know what to think. He was giving her no clues. 'Did you tell Nacho and Grace where we're going?' She dropped this in casually, but Kruz wasn't fooled.

'You don't get it out of me that way,' he said. 'Don't look so worried. We'll only be a few minutes away.'

All out of excuses, she poured the coffee.

'Smells good.'

Not half as good as Kruz, she thought, sipping

demurely as wild, erotic thoughts raged through her head. Kruz smelled amazing—warm, clean and musky man—and he was just so damn sexy in those snug-fitting jeans, with a day's worth of stubble and that bone-melting look in his eyes.

'I could go away again if you prefer,' he said, slanting her a dangerous grin to remind her just how risky it was to let her mind wander while Kruz was around. 'Come on,' he said, easing away from the counter. 'I'm an impatient man.' Dumping the rest of his coffee down the sink, he grabbed her hand.

'Shall I bring my camera?' she said, rattling her brain cells into line.

'No,' he said. 'If you can't live without recording every moment, I'll take some shots for you.'

He said this good-humouredly, but she realised Kruz had a point. She would relax more without her camera and take more in. Whatever Kruz wanted to show her was clearly important to him, and focusing a camera lens was in itself selective. She didn't want to miss a thing.

If she could concentrate on anything but Kruz, that was, Romy concluded as he helped her into her coat. It wasn't easy to shrug off the seductive warmth as his hands brushed her neck, her shoulders and her back. Kruz was one powerful opiate—and one she mustn't succumb to until she knew what this was about.

'So what now?' she said briskly as she locked up the penthouse.

'Now you have to be patient,' he warned, holding the door.

'I have to be *patient*?' she said.

Kruz was already heading for the stairs.

'Remember the benefits of delay.'

She stopped at the top of the stairs, telling herself that it was just a careless remark. It wasn't enough to stop fireworks going off inside her, but that was only because she hadn't thought about sex in a long time.

Today it occupied all her thoughts.

She was thrilled when Kruz drove them to the area of London she loved. 'You remembered,' she said.

He had drawn to a halt outside a gorgeous little mews house in a quaint cobbled square. It was just a short walk from the picturesque canal she had told him about.

'You haven't made any secret of your preferred area,' he said, 'so I thought you might like to take a look at this.'

'Do you own it?' she asked, staring up at the perfectly proportioned red brick house.

'I've been looking it over for a friend and I'd value your opinion.'

'I'd be more than happy to give it,' she said, smiling with anticipation.

And happy to dream a little, Romy thought as

Kruz opened the car door for her. There was nothing better than snooping around gorgeous houses—though she usually did it between the covers of a glossy magazine or on the internet. This was so much better. This was a dream come true. She paused for a moment to take in the cute wrought-iron Juliet balconies, with their pots of pink and white geraniums spilling over the smart brickwork. The property was south-facing, and definitely enjoyed the best position on the square.

She hadn't seen anything yet, Romy realised when Kruz opened the front door and she walked inside. 'This is gorgeous!' she gasped, struck immediately by the understated décor and abundance of light.

'The bedrooms are all on the ground floor,' he explained, 'so the upper floor can take advantage of a double aspect view over the cobbled square, and over the gardens behind the building. You don't think having bedrooms downstairs is a problem?'

'Not at all,' she said, gazing round. The floor was pale oak strip, and the bedrooms opened off a central hallway.

'There are four bedrooms and four bathrooms on this level,' Kruz explained, 'and the property opens onto a large private garden. Plus there's a garage, and off-street parking—which is a real bonus in the centre of London.'

'Your friend must be very wealthy,' Romy observed, increasingly impressed as she looked around.

'It's been beautifully furnished. I love the Scandinavian style.'

'My friend can afford it. Why don't we take a look upstairs? It's a large, open-plan space, with a kitchen and an office as well as a studio.'

'The studio must be fabulous,' she said. 'There's so much light in the house—and it feels like a happy house,' she added, following Kruz upstairs.

She gave a great sigh of pleasure when they reached the top of the stairs and the open-plan living room opened out in front of them. There were white-painted shutters on either side of the floor-to-ceiling windows, and the windows overlooked the cobbled square at one end of the room and the gardens at the other. Everywhere was decorated in clean Scandinavian shades: white, ivory and taupe, with highlights of ice-blue and a pop of colour played out in the raspberry-pink cushions on the plump, inviting sofa. Even the ornaments had been carefully chosen—a sparkling crystal clock and a cherry-red horse, even a loving couple entwined in an embrace.

'And there's a rocking horse!' she exclaimed with pleasure, catching sight of the beautifully carved dapple grey. 'Your friends are very lucky. The people who own this house have thought of everything for a family home.'

'And even if someone wanted to work from home here, they could,' Kruz pointed out, showing her the studio. 'Well?' he said. 'What do you think? Shall I tell my friend to go ahead and buy it?'

'He'd be mad not to.'

'Do you think we had better check the nursery before I tell him to close the deal?'

'Yes, perhaps we better had,' Romy agreed. 'At least I have some idea of what's needed in a nursery now.' She laughed. 'So I can offer my opinion with confidence.'

'Goodness,' she said as Kruz opened the door on a wonderland. 'Your friend must have bought out Khalifa's!' she exclaimed. Then, quite suddenly, her expression changed.

'Romy?'

Mutely, she shook her head.

'What is it?' Kruz pressed. 'What's wrong?'

'What's wrong,' she said quietly, 'is that it took me so long to work this out. But I got there eventually.'

'Got where? What do you mean?' Kruz said, frowning.

She lifted her chin. 'I mean, you got *me* wrong,' she said coldly. 'So wrong.'

'What are you talking about, Romy?'

'You bring me to a fabulous mews house in my favourite area of London because you think I can be bought—'

'No,' Kruz protested fiercely.

'No?' she said. 'You're the friend in question,

aren't you? Why couldn't you just be honest with me from the start?'

'Because I knew what you'd say,' Kruz admitted tersely. '*Dios*, Romy! I already know how pigheaded you are.'

'*I'm* pig-headed?' she said. 'You'll stop at nothing to get your own way.'

All he could offer was a shrug. 'I wanted this to be a surprise for you,' he admitted. 'I've never done this sort of thing before, so I just went ahead and did what felt right to me. I'm sorry if I got it wrong— got *you* wrong,' he amended curtly.

'Tell me you haven't bought it,' she said.

'I bought it some time ago. I bought it on the day I brought you home from hospital—which is why I had to leave you. I bought it so you and Beth would always have somewhere nice to live—whatever you decide about the future. This is your independence, Romy. This is my gift to you and to our daughter. If you feel you can't take it, I'll put it in Beth's name. It really is that simple.'

For you, she thought. 'But I still don't understand. What are you saying, Kruz?'

'What I'm saying is that I'm still not sure what you want, but I know what *I* want. I've known for a long time.'

'But you don't say anything to me—'

'Because you're never listening,' he said. 'Because

you haven't been ready to hear me. And because big emotional statements aren't my style.'

'Then change your style,' she said heatedly.

'We've both got a lot to learn, Romy—about loving and giving and expressing emotion, and about each other. We must start somewhere. For Beth's sake.'

'And that somewhere's here?' she demanded, opening her arms wide as she swung around to encompass the beautiful room.

'If you want it to be.'

'It's too much,' she protested.

'It isn't nearly enough,' Kruz argued quietly. Putting his big warm hands on her shoulders, he kept her still. 'Listen to me, Romy. For God's sake, listen to me. You have no idea what you and Beth have done for me. My nightmares have gone—'

'They've gone?' She stopped, knowing that nothing meant more than this. This meant they had a chance—Kruz had a chance to start living again.

'Baby-meds,' he said. 'Who'd have thought it?'

'So you can sleep at last?' she exclaimed.

'Through the night,' he confirmed.

It was a miracle. If she had nothing more in all her life this was enough. She could have kicked herself. She'd had baby-brain while Kruz had been nothing but considerate for her. The way he'd removed himself to give her space—the way he was always considerate with the keys, with Beth, with everything—the way he never hassled her in any way, or pushed her to make a decision. And had she listened to him? Had she noticed what was going on in his world?

'I'm so sorry—'

'Don't be,' he said. 'You should be glad—*we* should be glad. All I want is for us to be a proper family. I want it for Beth and I want it for you and me. I want us to have a proper home where we can live together and make a happy mess—not a showpiece to rattle round in like the penthouse. I don't think you want that either, Romy. I think, like me, you want to carry on what we started. I think you want us to go on healing each other. And I know I want you. I love you, and I hope you love me. I want us to give our baby the type of home you and I have always dreamed of.'

'And how will we make it work?' she asked, afraid of so much joy.

'I have no idea,' Kruz admitted honestly. 'I just know that if we give it everything we've got we'll make it work. And if you love me as much as I love you—'

'Hang on,' she said, her face softening as she dared to believe. 'What's all this talk of love?'

'I love you,' Kruz said, frowning. 'Surely you've worked that out for yourself by now?'

'It's nice to be told. I agree you're not the best when it comes to big emotional declarations, but you should have worked that out. Try telling me again,' she said, biting back a smile.

'Okay...' Pretending concentration, Kruz held her close so he stared into her eyes.

'I've loved you since that first encounter on the grassy bank—I just didn't know it then. I've loved you since you went all cold on me and had to be heated up again. I loved you very much by then.'

'Sex-fiend.'

'You bet,' he agreed, but then he turned serious again. 'And now I love you to the point where I can't imagine life without you. And whatever you want to call these feelings—' he touched his heart '—they don't go away. They get stronger each day. You're a vital part of my life now—the *most* vital part, since you're the part I can't live without.'

'And Beth?' she whispered.

'She's part of you,' Kruz said simply. 'And she's part of me too. I want you both for life, Señorita Winner. And I want you to be happy. Which is why I bought you the house—walking distance to the shops—great transport links...'

'You'd make an excellent sales agent,' she said over the thunder of her happy heart hammering.

'I must remember to add that to my CV,' Kruz teased with a curving grin. 'Plus there's an excellent nursery for Beth across the road.'

'Where you've already put her name down?' Romy guessed with amusement.

Kruz shrugged. 'I thought we'd live part of the year here and part on the pampas in Argentina. Whatever you decide the house is yours—or Beth's. But I won't let you make a final decision yet.'

'Oh?' Romy queried with concern.

'Not until you test the beds.'

'All of them?' She started to smile.

'I think we'd better,' Kruz commented as he swung her into his arms.

'Ah, well.' Romy sighed. 'I guess I'll just have to do whatever it takes…'

'I'm depending on it,' Kruz assured her as he shouldered open the door into the first bedroom.

'Let the bed trials begin,' she suggested when he joined her on the massive bed. 'But be gentle with me.'

'Do you think I've forgotten you've just had a baby?'

Taking her into his arms, Kruz made her feel so safe.

'What?' she said, when he continued to stare at her.

'I was just thinking,' he said, stretching out his powerful limbs. 'We kicked off on a mossy bank on the pampas beside a gravel path, and we've ended up on a firm mattress in your favourite part of London town. That's not so bad, is it?'

Trying to put off the warm honey flowing through her veins for a few moments was a pointless exer-

cise, Romy concluded, exhaling shakily with anticipation. 'Are you suggesting we work our way back
to the start?'

'If none of the beds here suit, I'm sure we can find
a grassy bank somewhere in the heart of London...'

'So what are you saying?' she whispered, shud-
dering with acute sexual excitement as Kruz ran his
fingertips in a very leisurely and provocative way
over her breasts and down over her belly, where they
showed no sign of stopping...

'I'm saying that if you can put up with me,' he
murmured as she exclaimed with delight and relief
when his hand finally reached its destination, 'I can
put up with you. I'm suggesting we get to know each
other really, really well all over again—starting at
the very beginning.'

'Now?' she said hopefully, surreptitiously easing
her thighs apart.

'Maybe we should start dating first,' Kruz said,
pausing just to provoke her.

'Later,' she agreed, shivering uncontrollably with
lust.

'Yes, maybe we should try the beds out first, as
we agreed...' Covering her hand with his, he held
her off for a moment. 'I'm being serious about us
living together,' he said. 'But I don't want to rush
you, Romy. I don't want to make you into something
you're not. I don't want to spoil you.'

'This house isn't spoiling me?' she said.

'Pocket change,' Kruz whispered, slanting her a bad-boy smile. 'But, seriously, I don't want to change anything about you, Romy Winner.'

'No. You just want to kill me with frustration,' she said. 'I can't believe you're suggesting we go out on dates.'

'Amongst other things,' he said.

'Then I'll consider your proposition,' she agreed, smiling against his mouth as Kruz moved on top of her.

'You'll do better than that,' he promised, in his most deliciously commanding voice.

'Just one thing,' she warned, holding him off briefly.

'Tell me...'

She frowned. 'I need time.'

'Does for ever suit you?' Kruz murmured, touching her in the way she liked.

'For ever doesn't really sound long enough to me,' she whispered against the mouth of the man she had been born to love.

EPILOGUE

IT WAS THE wedding of the year. Eventually.

It took five years for Kruz to persuade Romy that their daughter was longing to be a bridesmaid and that she shouldn't deny Beth that chance.

'So, for your sake,' she told her adorable quirky daughter, who was never happier than when she had straw in her hair and was wearing shredded jeans with a ripped top covered in hoof oil and horse hair, 'we're going to have that wedding you keep nagging me about, and you are going to be our chief bridesmaid.'

'Great,' Beth said, too busy taking in the intricacies of the latest bridle her father had bought her to pay much attention.

Kruz had finally managed to convince Romy that a wedding would be a wonderful chance to affirm their love, when to Romy's way of thinking she and Kruz already shared everything—with or without that piece of paper.

'But no frills,' Beth insisted, glancing up.

So she *was* listening, Romy thought with amusement. 'No frills,' she agreed—not if she wanted Beth for her bridesmaid.

And a slinky column wedding dress was out of the question for the bride as Romy was heavily pregnant for the third time. Kruz was insatiable, and so was she—more than ever now she was pregnant again. The sex-mad phase again. How lovely.

She felt that same mad rush of heat and lust when he strode into the bedroom now. Pumped from riding, in a pair of banged-up jeans and a top that had seen better times, he looked amazing—rugged and dangerous, just the way she liked him.

Who knew how many children they would have? Romy mused happily as Kruz swung Beth into the air. A polo team, at least, she decided as Kruz reminded their daughter that she was supposed to be going swimming with friends, and had better get a move on if she wasn't going to be late.

Leaving them to plan the wedding…or not, Romy concluded when he finally looked her way.

'The baby?'

She flashed a glance at the door of the nursery where their baby son was sleeping. 'With his nanny.'

She turned as Beth came by for a hug, before racing out of the room, slamming the door behind her. A glance at Kruz confirmed that he thought this was working out just fine. She did too, Romy concluded, taking in the power in his muscular forearms as Kruz propped a hip against her desk.

'Is this the guest list?' he asked, picking up the sheaf of papers Romy had been working on. 'You *do* know we only need two people and a couple of witnesses?'

'You have a big family—'

'And getting bigger all the time,' Kruz observed, hunkering down at her side.

'Who would have thought it?' Romy mused out loud.

'I would,' Kruz murmured wickedly. 'With your appeal and my super-sperm, what else did you expect?' He caressed the swell of her belly and then buried his head a little deeper still.

'I think you should lock the door,' she said, feeling the familiar heat rising.

'I think I should,' Kruz agreed, springing up.

He smiled as he looked down at her. 'I'm glad you lost those red-tipped gel spikes.'

'She frowned. 'What makes you bring those up?'

'Just saying,' Kruz commented with amusement, drawing her into the familiar shelter of his arms.

She had almost forgotten the red-tipped gel spikes. She didn't feel the need to present that hard, *stay-away-from-me* person to the world any more. And now she came to think about it losing the spikes hadn't been a conscious decision; it had been more a case of have baby, have man I love and have *so* much less time for me. And she wouldn't have it any other way.

'So, you like my natural look?' she teased as Kruz undressed her.

'I love you any way,' he said as she tugged off his top and started on his belt. 'Though the closer to nature you get, the more I like it...'

'Back to nature is best,' Romy agreed, reaching for her big, naked man as he tipped her back on the bed.

'Will I ever get enough of you?' Kruz murmured against her mouth as he trespassed at leisure on familiar territory.

'I sincerely hope not,' Romy whispered, groaning with pleasure as her nerve-endings tightened and prepared for the oh, so inevitable outcome.

'Spoon?' he suggested, moving behind her. 'So I can touch you...?'

Her favourite position—especially now she was so heavily pregnant. Arching her back, she offered herself for pleasure.

'Tell me again,' she told him much, much later, when they were lying replete on the bed.

'Tell you what again?' Kruz queried lazily, reaching for her.

'Do you *never* get enough?'

'Of you?' He laughed softly against her back. 'Never. So what do you want me to tell you?'

'Tell me that you love me.'

Shifting position, he moved so that he could see her face, and, holding her against the warmth of his body, he stared into her eyes. 'I love you, Romy Winner. I will always love you. This is for ever. You and me—we're for ever.'

'And I love you,' she said, holding Kruz's dark, compelling gaze. 'I love you more than I thought it possible to love anyone.'

'I especially love making babies with you.'

'You're bad,' she said gratefully as Kruz settled back into position behind her. 'You don't think…?'

'I don't think what?' he murmured, touching her in the way she loved.

'I'm expecting twins this time. Do you think it will be triplets next?'

'Does that worry you?'

She shrugged. 'We both love babies—just thinking we might need a bigger house.'

'Maybe…' he agreed. 'If we practise enough.'

She was going to say something, but Kruz had a sure-fire way of stopping her talking. And—*oh*… He was doing it now.

'No more questions?' he queried.

'No more questions,' she confirmed shakily as Kruz set up a steady beat.

'Then just enjoy me, use me. Have pleasure, baby,' he suggested as he gradually upped the tempo. 'And love me as I love you,' he added as she fell.

'That's easy,' she murmured when she was calmer, and could watch Kruz in the grip of pleasure as he found his own violent release. 'For ever,' she whispered as he held her close.

* * * * *